Sandman

Simon Humphreys

First published in 2015

by

RAGING AARDVARK PUBLISHING, Dalveen, Australia

http://ragingaardvark.com

Cover Image and *"Nets"*Image by Frances Jo Humphreys

Cover design by A Mitchell

DEDICATION

This book is dedicated to the fourth pea, Geoff...the only one who truly believed in me.

CONTENTS

CUP OF TEA

Half-drawn, heavy velvet curtains from bygone Blitzkrieg days wiped their feet on dusty, scratched parquet floors. The carpet's edge was tasselled through wear not design, and two pungent cotton-clad armchairs stood sentry duty either side of a three-legged coffee table; a grandson's gift from twenty years ago. The table had outlived its maker and his parents, but with another coat or two of paint, it would no doubt be good for a few more years.

The wallpaper that had once been so fashionable looked tired and longed to be stripped from the plaster it had covered for decades. One length had released itself from a damp and stained corner of the room, hanging its head in shame and resignation.

Both armchairs were occupied. One turned at an awkward angle, allowing its occupant fleeting glimpses of an outside world, which hurried about business beyond the dandelion garden and honeycomb half-brick wall.

The second chair snubbed the first and hogged the hearth, although there had been no warmth to covert, since the last four lumps of coal had refused to ignite with candle wax and cardboard.

Margaret had burned the tips of two fingers and thumb quite badly that day, attempting to coax the flaming card a little further under the heavy cast-iron grate. She'd been distracted by thoughts of the accident all those years ago and now, almost a week later, her poor fingers were tight and swollen, fit to burst their contents as readily as pork sausages sizzling in a pan.

"That table will be good for a few more years," she said, whilst using the back of her hand to straighten one of the white frilly lace chair covers, which concealed countless years of wear. "Another coat of paint and it'll be as good as new, you mark my words."

She gently scooped a mangy tabby cat from her lap and half placed, half dropped it to the floor, heaving a wheezy sigh with the effort.

Margaret was long past stretching her back on alighting her chair and long past dressing herself each day. Her green tracksuit pants, rose-patterned polyester dress and cotton dressing gown had kept her warm through the recent cold snap and, with no hot water, there was little else to change into, nor incentive to do so.

"You haven't finished your tea, George," she said, picking up a stone-cold cup and saucer with both hands. The skin on the back of her hands was smooth and phyllo-pastry thin. It was beyond wrinkled and bright blue veins were doing their best to surface. Her right hand trembled more than the left, which carried a simple gold wedding band, embedded deep into her flesh by the unsympathetic combination of time and fire.

"Can I get you another one, dear?"

With her throbbing left hand as support under the saucer, she gingerly tried to steady the cup with her shaking right wrist, as she shuffled from the lounge, spilling much of the cold brew into the saucer and from saucer to floor.

The passage leading from lounge to kitchen was once proudly fitted with woven wool carpeting of an even, light brown colour. It now mirrored the existence of the frail old lady, who daily shuffled and scuffed the pile flat and threadbare. The carpet was distinctly faded in a small triangular patch, constantly exposed to direct sunlight, and the large purple blotches with dark brown spots matched the taught skin that sheathed the thin, brittle bones of her hands.

Under the timber balustrade was a chest-high Victorian dresser, cluttered with china and an assortment of old family photos. Margaret paused and placed the cup next to a plastic cube, each face of which contained a small photo, the size of a beer mat. Caressing it gently in both hands, she stared blankly and briefly at the photo of Kevin, who was pictured standing proudly between grandparents; displaying his coffee table like some magnificent trophy on the day he'd visited them. He looked like she had always remembered him, happy and smiling, always smiling. Turning the cube slightly, she glanced at another photo, taken the same day, but this one had Kevin standing next to Margaret's only daughter and son-in-law. Father and son were dressed in matching tennis attire, although she didn't recall them having ever played the game. Nevertheless, they did look splendid, dressed all in white.

Taking an embroidered silk handkerchief from the sleeve of her gown, she gently wiped away the few specs of dust that had dared settle on the frames of her treasured memories, since she had last passed that way.

As she carefully picked up the saucer, a moist trail of cold tea smudged a path across the thin layer of dust that coated the dresser. A single teardrop fell from cheek to cup. Tea and tears became one, as Margaret slowly shuffled her open-heel slippers into the kitchen.

There was nowhere to place the saucer, other than one small corner of the kitchen table. The steel sink and two drainers were piled high with unwashed crockery, pots and even old emptied catfood tins. More tins littered the kitchen floor, some half-filled with grey candyfloss mould and others containing tea bags, or loose small change of varying denominations and currencies. Some held keys with no home whilst several small dead batteries were stored in another.

In the middle of the kitchen table, an old Sunday newspaper took pride of place. Spread-eagled from the centrefold, the paper was where a handful of cats ate their supper, which had been shovelled from tin to paper on countless previous occasions. The copy was illegible and scratched, as it served as both litter box and plate, to the dozen or more feral cats that roamed the house at will.

Between the steel sink and back door, a low-level ceramic pot sink was grouted onto a face-brick pedestal, testament to the previous house-owner's lack of building skills and taste. Above it, cold water constantly dripped from a chalk-encrusted bib tap. Margaret's contorted and disfigured fingers had lost their ability to firmly grip anything other than cupboard doors and catfood containers. Opening those tins was painful and tedious. The tap had remained turned off, but dripping for months; the life-giving drops being all she needed to fill the small, panel-beaten saucepan she placed beneath. It remained a permanent fixture under the tap … open-mouthed and grateful for every drop received.

The gas hob was functional, with only one of the four rings operational. The remaining three were used as storage space for redundant pots, vases, glassware and other receptacles, unable to be contained in the off-white cupboards, which were once white.

Margaret switched on the hob and at her third attempt managed to throw a lighted match into the gas. A small pile of used matches had built up in the space between metal gas ring and enamel hob. The light blue ring of fire ignited memories from deep within. No one had ever told them what had happened that day. Some suggested that Kevin may have been playing with matches, or perhaps an iron had been left switched on … an electrical fault, maybe. No one had ever told them.

The saucepan was full and had been for several hours. Margaret's shaking hand involuntarily reduced the level of water in the container, some disappearing down the drain and some splashing onto the linoleum tiles, most of which were slightly curled at the corners and brittle to cracking point. Fragments of loose flooring concentrated in areas of the kitchen that had been left undisturbed by shuffling feet, where they mingled with matted cat fur and discarded blue bottle pupae husks. Despite the spillage, there was still ample water in the pan for her requirements.

While the saucepan heated, the old cold tea was poured into the pot sink, leaving a dark brown ring around the perimeter of the cup. A mug was discovered on the windowsill next to the withered remnants of a desiccated pot plant of indiscernible species. Neither cup nor mug were clean, but into each was deposited a tea bag, carefully selected from the catfood tin on the table. Boiling water was shaken out of the saucepan onto newspaper, table top and floor, in equal quantities. Enough found its way into the cup and mug to ensure that drinks would be served and before the tea bags had been given time to brew for the second or third time, long-life milk was added from a carton. There was no sugar, but the tea was stirred vigorously with the same fork used for serving the cats. Steaming tea bags were retrieved and replaced in their tin until required to serve again.

Margaret paused, turned to the kitchen window and looked outside. Minutes passed, as the old lady stood transfixed and locked in a moment of time, from which she could not escape. There was nothing outside the kitchen window, nothing that would, or should have captured her attention in such an unrelenting grip. A plastered wall entirely filled the view through the window. It was unevenly rendered and had been only painted once that Margaret could remember.

She gazed at the peeling yellow wall, unable to recall the reason she was in the kitchen at all. She opened a kitchen cupboard door and then promptly closed it again, muttering a few words of self-admonishment in the process. The drawer beneath the cupboard then received the same treatment, as she frantically struggled to gather the loose reigns of her consciousness.

Turning back to the table, she picked up the saucepan and replaced it under the dripping tap once more. She stroked a small, flea-infested black-and-white kitten, which had scrambled up onto the table for the first time in its short life. The kitten's white whiskers were almost as long as her fingers. It stooped low, wiggled hind quarters back and forth … then pounced onto her outstretched hand, which she had placed next to her mug.

"Ah, the tea," she said confidently, picking up the mug in cupped hands and retracing her steps to the lounge.

Her tea was placed on the mantelpiece, before she returned to the kitchen, slowed this time by a sprightly Siamese, which weaved its slinky body with great skill and agility, in and out of her tiny steps.

Cups and saucers were so much more difficult to carry, although she coped with the mission without too much spillage, unhindered by cats and not allowing herself to be distracted by the photo gallery.

"There you go, George … a nice cup of tea for you."

Margaret placed the cup and saucer on Kevin's table and moved towards the mantelpiece. Her tea was now luke warm, but she sipped it as if it were piping hot. A few sips of tea were taken, before replacing the mug. She bent forward slightly and warmed her hands at the fire-less hearth, repeating her actions until finally she was sipping from an empty mug. No sooner had she sat down in her armchair, than a skinny black cat leapt up onto her lap. It clawed several times at Margaret's dressing gown, made three deliberate, slow revolutions of its chosen resting place and curled up for a nap.

Margaret didn't sleep, choosing to stroke the cat and gaze into the hearth. It would soon be spring and there would be no need for a fire. She found comfort in a small old-fashioned portable radio that played Big Band static next to her armchair. Unable to tune the dial effectively, she was content to leave it on a setting she had chanced upon some weeks ago. It was the music she enjoyed and the half-hourly inaudible news bulletins were of little interest or concern.

She wished her chair to be a rocking chair and her life to be another life; in another time. She thought of Kevin and how handsome he would be by now … a doctor, scientist, or teacher maybe. Just like his mother.

"You haven't finished your tea, George," she said. "Can I get you another one, dear?"

George neither answered her, nor did he finish his tea. He hadn't finished his tea that day, or the day before that.

Margaret made him another brew later that afternoon and yet again the next morning. Several hours later, she made another cup of tea and placed it on Kevin's table where it too, eventually went cold.

SANDMAN

The car door locked with a beep and Patrick filled his lungs with salty, crisp sea air. It was a perfect autumn morning and there was a real bite to it. His was one of three cars in the small municipal car park, the others no doubt belonging to pre-breakfast dog walkers. The sea was just visible through the early morning mist that lay like a thin gossamer blanket above the shore line.

Patrick stood and viewed the watercolour sandscape before him. It was called "long beach" for a reason. From the car park, for as far as he could see to his left, were two or three kilometres of pristine, sandy white perfection and beyond that another four or five. Pathways weaved randomly through grassy, low-lying sand dunes, beyond which lay a no man's land of dry, windswept, coarse sand. Once or twice a year the spring high tides and Atlantic storms would conspire to flush this flat, barren tundra clean and cough up substitute deposits of marine life and flotsam. A thin, hardened crust lay on the lunar surface, which broke underfoot, as would second-day snow or paper-thin puddle ice. Sticks entwined in fishing line, twisted coils of kelp tubes, crab claws and mussel shells littered the scene. A seagull's beak and one partially feathered skeletal wing projected from below, as if in a final desperate gesture for salvation.

It took only a few minutes for Patrick to pick his way across the pickled patch of land and reach the sea, which had eroded miniature cliffs into the compacted sand. He stood on the edge of the cliff. It collapsed under his weight, and sat him down softy on his backside. The heels of his trainers filled with sand, so he emptied them as he surveyed the scene before him. He'd never seen the sea so flat. Breaking waves were no more than ripples, that called out "shhh" to anyone who dared break the silence. Not even the gulls dared do that.

"Shhh ... shhh ... shhh ..." Whispered the sea and Patrick obeyed.

Taking his wide-brimmed white cotton hat, Patrick brushed the sand from the seat of his shorts and walked the few paces down to the water's edge. A frontline of green frothy slime moved in and out with the sea and beyond that, patches of kelpshake foam floated undisturbed on the surface of the grey water, which mirrored the hazy, but cloudless sky. Patrick took a step back to avoid soaking his trainers. He tap-danced the toe of his shoe on the glistening saturated sand, which brought water to the surface in a small puddle that caused droplets of sand to splash his other ankle.

He walked the shoreline; a solitary figure in the wide, open space. In the distance, but way off towards the dunes, he spotted one of the dog walkers, but dog and owner were no more than ants on the horizon. His thoughts were of better times, of days not so long ago

… carefree days before what he called the "dark pain" that had taken over his life, increasing in intensity and frequency.

He stopped at one point and crouched down on his haunches, holding the palms of his hands to his temples and squeezing as hard as he could. It felt as though the back of his skull was being branded through his eyeballs by two white-hot pokers. This was the dark pain; the pain that shut out all other thoughts and swallowed his very being, down through a screaming vortex and into the darkest depths of hell.

They said that if he was strong and fought hard, he could "beat it". They said a lot of things, but what did they know?

After a time, Patrick opened his eyes. The pain had eased a little and he squinted into the bright light. He was on his hands and knees in the moist sand. With his forefinger and no forethought, he wrote two letters in the sand, with a gap in between. The letters "P" and "K" spelt out his name, but with a large part missing. He didn't know why he wrote it, or why it was incomplete. It was just an involuntary act, like many others in his recent life.

The walk continued for more than an hour. Patrick turned and walked backwards for a couple of minutes, casting his eyes back down the single line of footsteps in the sand. They pointed back towards the car-park end of the beach, which had completely disappeared from view. He turned and resumed his walk, following the line of the breaking ripples. A dark figure in the sand grew closer and Patrick correctly guessed it to be that of a seal carcass long before any defining features could be seen. A feeling of nausea welled up within, as the sandflea covered corpse of a silver seal pup greeted him. A seagull stood nearby nonchalantly looking the other way, like a 1940s' spiv accused of peddling contraband stockings or tins of condensed milk.

Patrick could have looked away from the rotting animal, or given it a wide berth, but instinctively he walked within a pace or two, glancing down without breaking stride. Sweet saliva filled his mouth. He spat towards the sea and then spat again. His eyes were bloodshot and watery and his skin became clammy and sweaty, as the sun began to dissolve the remnants of the early-morning mist. He removed his hat and wiped his wet, hairless head with the front of his T-shirt, revealing his skinny torso; more ribs than flesh and a sickly greenish hue – not dissimilar to that of the kelp froth that lined the shore.

Behind him was nothing but sand and sea; ahead of him kilometres of the same. He sat down to rest and placed his hat to one side for company, having first built a little pillow mound of sand behind the small of his back for support. His legs were spread and knees were bent ... on each he rested an elbow. Once more he crafted an image in the sand. A large circle formed a face and a squiggle gave it a button nose in the centre. He tried to draw a "smiley" but his finger shook as he placed it in the soft wet sand at what should have been the corner of a mouth. At best he would scratch a straight line across the face. He closed his eyes and when he reopened them, he saw a sad blind man with an upturned smile. He plunged a finger deep into the sand and created an eye. Another stab of his digit drew a slight wince and expletive, as his finger caught the sword-like edge of a buried mussel shell, deep within the brain of his imaginary friend. The cut was deep and blood dripped from the end of his sandy finger. He flicked it and droplets of red splattered the golden sand beyond his hat.

The stony face in the sand glared back at him, angered at being created in the image of a morose Charlie Brown. Patrick punched his fist deep into Charlie's nose, then scooped handfuls of forehead over his shoulder. Frantically he dug away at the head of the image, shifting the excavated face over his shoulder.

"They said this would help," he muttered to himself. "What do they know?"

He stopped digging, as he once more encountered the offending mussel shell, though this time no blood was shed as he struck it full on broadside with the tips of two fingers.

In the time that he had been there, the tide had noticeably retreated some distance. The far end of the beach was lifeless and barren, but as he peered back towards the car park, a matchstick man appeared out of the haze in the distance. Patrick watched as the stranger came closer, only taking his eyes off the intruder to roll his head and click a few aching neck vertebrae back into order. The stranger was also dressed in shorts and his semi-formal buttoned shirt was neatly tucked into them. From twenty metres, the grey hair, walking stick and measured gait placed him in his late sixties, or seventies.

Without a word, the stranger carefully lowered himself and sat on the nearest, hatless side of Patrick. They both looked out towards the horizon and an eternity passed in silence, both men paying homage to the call of the sea, which whispered to them. "Shhh … shhh."

The two men engaged in conversation, eventually finding an affinity with one another. The stranger listened and seemed to understand. He agreed with Patrick when the younger man said, "What do they know?" and he gestured a nod of approval when the disfigured image of Charlie was explained to him. Patrick told him of the "dark pain" and the burning bitterness he harboured within. He turned to the stranger; as the stranger turned to him. They looked deep into each other's eyes. They were similar in mind and would have been similar in body, if those bodies were not separated by a generation, or more. The old man was a stranger no more. The two men talked on and listened intently to one other. They agreed that the sea was unusually calm and beckoning that day. The older man suggested that Patrick may cool the fire that raged within by heeding the call of the sea, which could cleanse the soul and heal a broken spirit.

His friend would remain on the beach and ensure his belongings were safe, as Patrick seemed concerned that his driver's licence and credit-card identity not be stolen. He told the old man that his earliest seaside memories were of "stripping down to my underpants on Whitstable's rounded pebble shoreline and gingerly …"

"… Hobbling down into the dark grey waters of the Thames estuary." The old man finished his sentence for him, word for word, precisely as they had formed in Patrick's mind, just moments before.

Patrick placed his trainers on the sand, followed by car keys, wallet and watch. Shorts and shirt were neatly folded and topped off with his white cotton hat. He then sat down again in the same spot, neatly fitting into the little indentation in the sand that was his seat. He turned to his friend and instinctively lifted his left hand to the air, as if to bid farewell. The old man mirrored the action and for a brief moment their hands almost met … barely inches apart.

"Go," said the friend. "Go … as far as you need to and for as long as it takes. Go, my friend, go."

Patrick stood and blinked dry the tears that welled in his eyes. He walked the twenty steps to the sea, which was calling, but taunting him in its slow retreat. The Atlantic had a numbing effect on his feet, as he strode deeper into its arms. His progress was unflinching and soon he was wading waist-deep into the icy ocean.

There were no waves to battle and the salty water seemed to warm in his path, as he eased his way out beyond the froth and into deeper seas. The further he went, the better he would feel. His friend had assured him of that and he believed it now more than ever. He would purge the "dark pain" and put out the fires of hell. He looked back at the beach once more. It was far away and was slowly becoming another misty horizon. The sky above was a bright white light, as was the sea, which glinted and blinked as it bounced the sun around like a beach ball. The land beyond the beach was also becoming blinding and blurred, as a fine white veil lowered itself before his eyes. He turned once more ... tired, but determined. His body was weak, but his mind was strong. "Fight it." That's what they had said. "Go on ... fight ... go on and on."

"Who do you think these belong to, Daddy?" shouted the shrill little voice, as the dainty young girl skipped ahead of her mother and father, pointing to the footsteps in the sand.

"I don't know, Pixie," he replied. "Who do you think it is?"

"Robinson Crusoe." she cried.

"Could be ... could be."

"Well now he's walking backwards, looking for his friend, Friday."

"So he is," her father chuckled.

They followed the tracks past the dead seal pup and the gull that had edged close to its open jaws. The little girl leapt from footprint to footprint, her tiny strides unable to match those of her prey.

"Looks like another dead seal up ahead," said the man to his wife. "Look out, Pixie, there may be another seal over there." His daughter thought not and shouted as much back to her father.

The small family gathered just short of the neat little bundle of clothes, upon which lay a wide-brimmed white hat. The solitary set of footprints ended at the parcel of clothes and the small patch of disturbed sand. A little closer to the sea, someone had drawn a circle, from which another set of barefoot prints led into the sea. There were no footprints returning from the ocean and the young couple looked at each other, as the reality of the situation dawned. Their daughter wanted to know where Robinson had gone and was relieved to hear that he had probably swam out to a rescue boat, which had plucked him from the water and taken him to safety.

The girl's father picked up the hat and unbundled the clothes. His wife looked further down the beach and confirmed that there were no footprints beyond their own and those of the man who had been there before them. They opened the wallet and an identity was revealed. Pixie played with a dead crab, as her father put his arms around his wife and held her close. She hesitated for a second, before she read aloud the details of the owner of the driving licence she held in her hand.

"Patrick Matthews, date of birth 6 June 1976. Jesus, he is … was

… is only in his thirties."

The parcel of clothes and other belongings were placed in the wife's beach bag and taken back to the car park and from car park to police station. By mid-afternoon, the tale was being retold to officers, who then relayed it to emergency and welfare services. Welfare informed relatives, who in turn, phoned friends.

The sea rediscovered its voice, reclaimed the land and erased the footprints. It wiped Charlie's face clean and washed the droplets of blood from the grains of sand. The seal pup carcass lasted longer, but eventually succumbed to time and tide.

Pixie told classmates of her day at the beach and how she followed in the footsteps of Robinson Crusoe. Her parents told their friends a different version of the same story and later that week they solemnly read the following in the classified section of their local newspaper:

"Patrick Matthews 6 June 1976 – 25 May 2012. Beloved husband of Linda and father to James and Catherine. We will miss you more than you will ever know, but now you can rest in peace. May the angels watch over you, darling. Memorial service at St. Joseph's Church.

No flowers please, but donations if you wish to the Institute of Cancer Research."

Sandman : in memory of Tony Potter

SERVICE DELIVERY

The road was black and sticky-toffee hot as the sun tried to melt the premix surface. A shimmering layer of heat floated knee high, disturbed only by the occasional passing of a soft-drinks truck. There was no wind to move the air, which hung dry and dusty under the cloudless molten white sky. Thandeka's bare feet were as tough as rhino hide, having never worn shoes, yet she chose to walk the uneven gravel footpath rather than cook her soles on the smooth, but baking road.

It was not just Thandeka's feet that bore a hardness beyond their years. At barely fifteen, she had long lost the looks deserved of one her age. Slim and petite, with peppercorn hair, her teak-toned skin was pimpled and bumpy. She once possessed a beaming smile and sparkling eyes, that lit up her face when she giggled and played with the other township children. Her smile was now gone, unseen for months and locked away forever. Her eyes were sad, milky coffee in colour and totally bloodshot – lacking hope, revealing nothing and completely emotionless.

She paused to adjust the burden she carried on her back. Bending down, she balanced the baggage, whilst untying the blanket that held it in place. The baggage cried a little, then sporadically whimpered, but sensing the futility, closed her eyelids and gently returned to a place where there was no hunger or pain and mother's breasts were rich with milk. Thandeka tied the knot tight, arched her aching back as much as she could. She looked skyward, directly into the blinding sun. Her lips were cracked and parched, but there would be no relief for her thirst until she reached the clinic, some five kilometres on from here. She ran her tongue across her top lip, feeling her way over the roughened surface, catching a loose, flaky piece, which half lifted, half dangled.

It would be another two hours before she reached the clinic, such was the pace of her progress. There was no shade or shelter in the barren landscape and no soothing cool stream to relieve her swollen feet or cool her salty brow.

She had been walking for an hour and in that time only a handful of vehicles had passed her by. It was too risky to hitch, and there was precious little chance of anyone stopping for a young mother and child, with anything but evil intentions. It had happened before and it would happen again. Lips, noses, eyes and genitals were prized body parts for making "muti" and although never openly discussed in the village, everybody knew of such dangers and feared for the lives of their children.

Thandeka hummed a little song to relieve the tedium and take her mind off her hunger and thirst, occasionally breaking into song, when her baby began to weep. By mid-afternoon, she had reached the outskirts of the small town and trudged the last few hundred metres up a steep hill to the local clinic, which offered medicine and food to all in need. Being the only clinic in the area, it served a multitude of villages and small townships and there were many in need that day and every day, six days a week.

It was Thandeka's second visit to the clinic with Nomvula, having previously brought her baby there three months ago, when the child was merely six weeks old. On that occasion her grandmother had accompanied her, just to show her the way and to keep an eye on the oldest of six grandchildren in her care.

The first journey had seemed far less gruelling and certainly much cooler. This time she felt drained and completely overwhelmed with the whole experience. Nomvula had hardly gained any weight in the intervening months, so it was most probably the heat of the day and lack of company that had accounted for her exhaustion. Thandeka's grandmother had given her all she could afford, to buy a little food, or in case of an emergency. The ten rand she pressed into her granddaughter's fist had been earned from selling little brightly coloured animal beadwork, which was collected from the local women and sold on street corners, or the gift shops of big towns and cities far away. Her speciality was miniature lions, about the size of a matchbox, used as key rings or merely hung as ornaments from rear-view car mirrors.

The clinic was an old residential detached house from the 1930s which had recently been converted. A complete alteration of the existing building, combined with a modern extension, courtesy of some much-needed Danish Christian aid, had doubled the size of the original dwelling, but totally destroyed any architectural merit that may have existed prior to the conversion.

The long queue that greeted Thandeka and her baby had not been unexpected. The line of forty or more people snaked its way from the entrance door of the clinic, out onto what had once been a front garden. A haphazard and slow-moving queue, which at one point doubled back on itself for no apparent reason, leaving the tale-enders facing the town with their backs to the clinic.

Thandeka didn't really know why she was there. Her grandmother had sent her, saying that Nomvula was not well and needed medicine. The baby was small and cried a lot, but other than that, Thandeka thought she was like all the other babies she had seen in the village.

Thandeka viewed the line of people that twisted like the roadkill cobra she had seen that day … how it resembled that snake she had approached with caution and then kicked into the veld, upon realising it was dead. She hated snakes. Not only was the twisted queue outside the clinic motionless, but it was filled with the old, sick and barely living. There were men staring deep down into the ground, bent double with the weight of time, supporting their frail bodies on walking sticks made from branches. A grandmother sat on an upturned beer crate, her grandson holding aloft a black umbrella for shade, she was barely able to raise it above her head. There were many mothers with babies, just like her own Nomvula, strapped to backs, unable to move.

Thandeka quickened her pace as she passed the queue, not wishing to join it further back than she needed to. First, she needed to drink from the dripping tap on the wall outside a detached block containing two toilets. She lay Nomvula down on the ground next to the brick-filled puddle that was a permanent water feature below the tap. A dead rat lay nearby, giving birth to a family of maggots, and a deposit of excrement played host to dozens of swarming flies. She washed her baby's face as best she could and trickled a little liquid into her open mouth with the aid of a cupped hand. Then she placed her head under the tap and ran it full bore, shaking a shower of droplets over her daughter. The water was tepid but so good, as she took her fill directly from the plastic spout of the tap.

Her thirst satisfied, Thandeka strapped her baby to her back once more and walked slowly back past the queue of other mothers, where more flies feasted on streaming noses and swollen eyelids gummed closed with yellow paste.

There she stood, at the tail of a dead snake, not knowing anyone, deep in thought, caring not to waft away insects, nor the demons that welled within, constantly reminding her of that night when against her will, she had been taken into the veld for some "fun". She glanced around once more. There were no such people in her queue that day. Just old men; sad old men … no young men. Good … no young men. She felt glad looking at the sad old men.

Several more people joined the line behind her, as the snake rose from the dead and shuffled a few metres forward, before lapsing once more into a coma. It was painfully slow, but there was no hurry. Thandeka had expected to be sleeping rough that night after the clinic had closed. She would find a safe patch of open ground and cuddle her baby to sleep in a cocoon of body and blanket. But for now, she must be patient and content to be one of the vertebrae in the middle of the snake, moving as its body moves, slowly winding its way towards the clinic.

Thandeka noticed a kindly looking woman, not dissimilar to her own grandmother, walking slowly along the queue from the direction of the clinic. She was talking to all the mothers with babies, taking her time and looking concerned, as if personally involved in the plight of each poor soul waiting their turn. She was a strong woman, who obviously knew about the ways of the world. Her voice was loud, but calm. Perhaps she was a doctor from the clinic, just venturing out to see if all was well in the outside world.

She caught Thandeka's eye. The young girl looked down instinctively, too shy to hold her ground and not wishing to stare at the clever doctor from the clinic.

The doctor reached Thandeka and paused at the girl's side. She introduced herself as Vumile and told the girl not to worry about her child. The clinic had very good medicine, which would make her baby strong again. She too had a granddaughter Thandeka's age and she was sure that not so long ago she had visited the very village that Thandeka had left that morning.

Vumile chatted for some time and was of great comfort, with her words of wisdom and reassuring manner. She may even have met Thandeka's grandmother on her travels, because when she was told the old lady's name, she immediately remembered meeting someone by that name. It was indeed a very small world and Thandeka apparently reminded Vumile of that lady in so many ways.

There appeared to be a little more life in the snake, as it slithered ever closer to its destination. But with still some way to go, Thandeka's stomach reminded her that she had not eaten since early that morning and the energy provided by her breakfast of cold mealie pap had been expended hours ago. Nomvula had drunk what breast milk was available, but Thandeka really needed to replenish herself. There was a small spaza shop some fifty metres away, where she could purchase a loaf of bread and a carton of milk with less than the money she had been given. However, she didn't know if the other women would let her re-join the snake if she left now. She didn't know any of them. Perhaps they would turn against her.

Vumile noted her anxiety and offered to take her place in the queue, while she went to fetch food. Thandeka could trust Vumile. She hadn't said she was a doctor from the clinic, but she was kind and friendly. She even knew Thandeka's grandmother.

Vumile said that Thandeka looked tired, which was no surprise, as she'd been carrying Nomvula all day. Her aching bones needed a rest and Vumile suggested the baby be left with her in the queue. She would be quite safe.

Thandeka untied the blanket from around her waist and handed Nomvula and blanket to Vumile. The kind lady eased back the blanket, which was partly covering the baby's face, and stroked the silky smooth skin with the back of her hand. Vumile cradled the still sleeping infant in her arms and rocked her gently to and fro, whispering a simple lullaby onto the crown of the small child's head. "Tula tu, tula baba, tula sana."

The bread and milk were bought from the spaza and Thandeka returned to the snake, instinctively looking along the portion closest to the clinic. She quickly scanned the complete line again from head to toe and back again, quickening her step as the adrenalin pumped through her veins. As she reached the meandering queue of lost souls, she ran to the front, spinning one old lady off her feet as she grabbed her shoulder, believing it be that of Vumile. "Eish!" the woman cried as she regained her balance.

Thandeka prowled the line, up and down, until she reached the place where she had left her baby. The woman who had been standing behind her stopped her frantic pacing. Within seconds a commotion ensued, as slowly the realisation dawned on the gathering that Vumile had calmly walked away with the baby, as soon as Thandeka had entered the spaza. Nobody had thought anything of it. Surely Thandeka knew her well. They seemed to know each other very well and, after all, it hadn't been a case of grab and run. She simply walked away.

Women were shouting and screaming. Thandeka raced off in one direction, only to return and run in another. She tripped and fell not far from the crowd, face down in the dirt with outstretched hands and bleeding palms. She remained there sobbing, her tiny body heaving uncontrollably, before being helped inside the clinic by one of the staff, who had rushed outside to investigate the reason for the noise. Inside the building, Thandeka was given a hot cup of tea. She helped herself to six spoons of sugar, spilling an equal amount onto the table, as her hands and whole body shook violently.

It was relatively quiet in the clinic, but absolute bedlam outside, as people shouted and fought with each other, over where they had been in the queue before it disintegrated into such chaos. Two women were pulling at the clothes of another, whilst the third had picked up the black umbrella. She used the seemingly innocuous object to jab an old lady back to where she believed she belonged, at the tail end of the invisible snake.

The police were called and an hour later two young constables arrived at the clinic. One of the men had a notebook and scribbled furiously, whilst the other asked questions of everyone who had witnessed the incident. There was no shortage of witnesses to interview. Everyone had seen exactly what had happened. A young man had grabbed the baby and sped off in a BMW. He was probably going to sell it to a witchdoctor for "muti." Another claimed the young girl arrived at the clinic alone and was lying to the police about her baby … she didn't have one. Then there were a few people who actually gave the correct version, which was of little help to the besieged policemen. "She was about fifty, no seventy … a large woman, but not very big … like that woman there, or maybe that one."

The next day, the news of the baby snatcher at the clinic made national news on the radio. A reporter had interviewed Thandeka at the clinic not long after the incident. She had been given a decent meal and a lift back home to her village the same evening. Over the next few days, national news became local and after two weeks the police had no further information on the missing baby. Nomvula was slowly becoming a statistic, forgotten by all but her immediate family.

Thandeka became an even sadder, more reclusive young girl, avoiding the people of the village, who whispered things she could not hear and, despite the best efforts of her grandmother, she feared that her little Nomvula was gone forever.

Many miles away, in one of the big cities by the sea, where people lived in houses taller than trees, a middle-aged woman walked her yappy little Jack Russell among the many cloth-covered trestle tables that displayed their goods at the Sunday craft market. She wore a jacket that matched in colour that of her dog. The animal's waistcoat which was a knitted woollen creation, bought mail order through the "Puppy Parlour". The woman's body-hugging cerise jacket was made by one of the city's leading design houses, and the jacket was in shocking contrast to her long auburn hair, which was showing flashes of grey along a centre parting.

She wasn't accustomed to browsing in craft markets, preferring the exclusive shops of top-notch malls. Irritated with herself at being drawn to this destination, she walked tall and with purpose, gliding through the milling crowd, which parted like obedient biblical seas before a greater presence. In her wake, an elderly maid tried as best she could to keep up with her employer, eager to take advantage of the open path before her, before it closed again. It was not easy, as the wheels of the pram she pushed, either caught on isolated tufts of grass or molehills, or locked in little potholes and depressions in the ground.

The woman paused at a stall, which was selling trinkets and jewellery made from indigenous materials. Not interested in the cheap earrings, bracelets, or malachite pendants, she picked up a small, but eye-catching item, about the size of a matchbox. She tied the dog's leash to the exposed leg of the display table and bent down over the pram. The maid instinctively took a pace back. Peeling back the soft pink blanket, the woman placed the little lion crafted from a multitude of brightly coloured beads on the sleeping baby's chest. She covered the ornament with the blanket, untied the dog and stood up tall and straight, pleased with her purchase, but not pleased enough to suggest even a flicker of a smile.

"There," she said, gingerly patting the handle of the pram. "I think it's time to go home."

The maid nodded approvingly, but said nothing. She regained possession of the pram and rocked it a little … very gently, before falling in line behind the dog, and the woman in the smart jacket.

As she walked, the maid sang a little song to herself and the baby …. "Tula tu, tula baba, tula sana."

TRENCHES

The "Tommy" infantryman lay spread-eagled and nose down against the battered face of the sandy embankment, that formed the only barrier between him and the kiss of an enemy bullet to the forehead. The partially completed trench had only been started that day and its depth barely matched his height, the minimum requirement for a night on the front line. He turned his head to one side and glimpsed the sky above. The cloudy, moonless night offered up no more light than the face of the trench, viewed through tightly closed eyes. It was a warm, windless night; too warm for visible breath, eased out between chapped, pursed lips, from deep within the young man's chest. He stifled a cough.

A silence filled the air, where once was mustard gas, dark grey smoke and muted cries of pain. The soldier waited for the inevitable onslaught from enemy lines. He took back his breath from the night and filled his lungs. He'd practised in the bath at home and now he practised on the front. He'd try to make the count to forty, even fifty. It may save his life … it may not.

A flash of light in the distance heralded the arrival of the first wave of heavy artillery bombardment destined for their positions. Seconds later it would be upon them … upon him, spreading death, dispersing limbs, mud, timber and metal like devil's confetti over the barren wasteland. The Tommy did not know what to expect, as this was his first day on the line, in his trench.

When it came it was like nothing he had prepared himself for. He'd dreamt of little else for the past few weeks, but this was so much louder and on a bigger scale than even he had imagined.

The first explosion felt like it was no more than a foot from his ear drums. Then another, followed by a second or two of peace, before all hell broke loose. Explosions so loud and frequent that they were almost indistinguishable from one another; a cacophony of brain-shattering, earth-lifting noise. He covered his ears with his palms and buried his head in the embankment.

He told himself to fight the fear, but nausea welled up from within, at the thought of what lay ahead. He lifted his head just enough to peer over the wall of his trench. The darkness gave protection enough from enemy snipers; more protection than offered by his tin hat and reflexes.

High above him, sulphurous explosions cast eerie shadows on the ground. Moving lights in the sky, gave birth to sinister creatures on the ground. Tree-stump silhouettes and broken fence posts became enemy foot soldiers advancing on his position. To his left, a direct hit on a munitions storage depot sent fiery red-and-green serpents screaming skyward in every direction, before they too fell still and cold on the battle ground. The shadow men fell with them and for a few brief moments darkness swallowed the entire landscape.

In front of him, shells detonated every other second, rearranging vast swathes of no man's land into pitted lunar backdrops with barbed-wire protrusions and steaming clods of thick brown mud.

The Tommy strained his eyes to the horizon, scanning every outcrop, every hollow for signs of movement, telltale twitches of adrenalin-charged foot soldiers eager to steal an inch of his land. A nearby explosion sent him scurrying deep into his trench as fine sand rained down like the icing-sugar coating on his grandmother's birthday cakes.

As he waited for the final call, a knot formed in the pit of his stomach. He couldn't be sick, not here in his trench. What would be said of the new boy in the trench, coughing up his cowardly sick? He would show them. He popped his head up and fired off a single round into the wasteland, before ducking back down under cover. A grenade was ripped from his belt, pin extracted, seconds counted and then lobbed overhead from his position at the bottom of the trench. He heard the explosion and only hoped that it had landed somewhere out there, nearer them and not in some godforsaken shell hole … hell hole; filled with other poor souls from his own frontline.

In the distance, the high-pitched tingle of a bicycle bell drifted over his trench and continued for a minute or two, until it faded away some distance behind his lines. Perhaps it was a party of those stretcher bearers that he'd heard so much about; but did they have bells? He couldn't think what else it may be, but comforted himself in the knowledge that others were out there, bravely doing their duty. In return for their courage, they could expect a shorter than normal stint on the front than most. Stretcher bearers were often sent home sooner than others … in a body bag, shoe box, or just a standard-issue army letter, depending on just how much of them was found in the mud and sludge of the land they patrolled.

A shot rang out from his position, then another. Someone down the line screamed a stomach-churning wail, which gurgled and then faded away on the back of another shell blast. Would that be his scream, if and when his time came? Would he go slowly, or would a sniper pick him out in the rock-steady cross hairs of his rifle? The frequency of the shell blasts intensified, as did their volume. They were getting closer, too close.

Someone leapt into his trench from behind the lines and landed halfway up his calf, heels scraping down the side of his leg and across his ankle. He withdrew his foot and wanted cry out, but just grimaced into his sleeve. It was a fleeting visit from the other soldier, who immediately scampered off along the trench and out of sight without a word.

"Come on, Tommy, come on," came the voice from behind. "It's time to go. It's time to go. Go, go, go." Those were the words he had waited for and dreaded. He knew they were coming, but as he heard them, his body froze. His eyes welled with the salty wetness of suppressed tears. His muscles ached and his head was spinning, as orders were barked out to him once again.

"Tommy, this is it. We must go. It's way past your time," came the same voice, increasing in intensity.

He heard himself cry out loud "No! Not now, not now ... I can't."

Fear and panic gripped every muscle and sinew in his body.

"Tommy!"

"No, no, no," he cried, but it was useless protesting and he knew it. The consequences of not obeying such orders were well known and he blocked his mind against such thoughts.

"Thomas! If you don't come now, then there will be no next time," shouted the voice, echoed by another pleading with him in the same manner.

"Thomas!"

Without warning, the little soldier was lifted off his feet and up into the air by an irresistible force. He felt the end was upon him and he knew the game was up.

"Honestly, Thomas, we said that you could stay up till eight o'clock and it's half past that already. You've got school tomorrow, you know."

The young boy was still light enough to be carried fireman fashion over the shoulders of his father, down the promenade of Fish Hoek beach and off towards the car. He protested and cried, but to no avail, as he viewed the throng of people remaining on the beach; big boys much older than himself, throwing bangers, lighting jumping jacks and setting off their rockets – sticks stuck loosely in the sand, or protruding from discarded Coke tins. His eyes grew heavy as he traced the flight of a Roman candle, which sent bright red-and-green serpents screeching high into the sky.

A thunder flash exploded close by and little further down the beachfront pathway, a man on a tricycle sold ice creams from a box strapped neatly between the handlebars. He rang his bell to summon potential customers, but the little soldier was too battle weary to cry out for a treat.

His mother walked along side, running her fingers through his mop of blond locks. She wiped sand from his cheeks with a spit-moistened tissue, then a few more specks from the tip of his nose.

A small telltale trail of sand sprinkled the pavement, as the boy's tight grip was slowly released from his recently formed sand grenade. He muttered "no" a couple of times and then closed his eyes.

"He's gone already," his mother whispered. "That was quick … out like a light, before we even reached the car. At least he's enjoyed himself on his first-ever proper fireworks night. Did you see him out there ... in a world of his own?"

Thomas' father nodded in agreement. "I certainly did. I wonder what on earth goes through his mind sometimes. But I still don't get it. Why do we have a fireworks night in South Africa? Isn't it a British thing?"

ALICE

Vertical shadows thrown against the bright white wall, framed in the soft warm light of an early-morning sunrise. As the box of light slowly inches its way down from the top of the wall, the intensity of the rising sun gradually lights up the room. There are no curtains to dampen the impact of the morning … only internal mild steel burglar bars, hinged on one side and padlocked the other. The heavy sections of the unpainted bars cast the shadows and, across them, welded steel rods protect the teak sash window glazing from clenched fists and bare wrists.

Alice watches and waits for the rectangular light to drift downward and sink into the wall and solid steel door, as the full light of dawn reveals a cloud-free spring morning. Her cast-iron bed and foam mattress occupy a corner opposite the door, whilst a toilet and sink designate the bathroom in another corner. A small pine coffee table completes the furniture inventory, and painted concrete floors do little to ease the cold starkness of the room. Alice is huddled in the corner at the head of the bed, clutching a block of foam between her knees and chest. Her arms lock her legs in place, as she rocks back and forth rhythmically. She peers over the top of her pillow, biting down deep into the sponge, which sucks the saliva from her cheeks.

That is how they had found Alice almost twenty years before, slowly rocking her petite frame back and forth, whilst clutching her knees to her chest. Emily was on the kitchen floor; her skull cracked open like the shell of the cold boiled egg above her on the baby's high chair. Four toast soldiers lay next to the tiny body, one dipped in a thin veneer of congealed yolk, the others thick with dark brown clotted blood. In the children's room, four-year old James lay motionless in his bed, his face still covered with the blue-and-white striped cotton blanket.

Many of the local population of Aston had called for the noose, but no woman had been hanged in Britain for nearly ten years. Alice maintained her innocence at the outset of her trial, but as the proceedings progressed, she withdrew from the reality of the situation and spoke in almost inaudible whispers. By the time the judge passed sentence, she hadn't uttered a word for weeks.

Rampton Secure Hospital opened its doors to Alice in 1964. It had no intention of ever opening them again for her.

A set of keys being sorted outside her door told Alice that her daily routine was about to begin; the same way it had begun for the past seven thousand days. An eye-level viewing slot in the door was opened and slammed shut in double-quick time. The wrong key was put into the escutcheon, then another. Finally, the correct key opened the lock and the heavy steel door pushed wide open by the flat-soled shoes of a fat-arsed nurse, who kept her distance in the doorway.

"Come on, Alice, what are you doing over there? Come and eat something ... there's a good girl."

The "something" was placed on the coffee table by the nurse, who then retraced her steps backwards to the doorway. The meal comprised an apple, a hardboiled egg, a carton of milk and a large bowl of cornflakes. The bowl was plastic, as was the spoon – deemed safe to leave ... unlike the metal tray, which the nurse clasped close to her chest with one arm, as she locked the door behind her.

Alice just stared ahead at the wall opposite her bed, unmoved by thoughts of breakfast, or the visit she would receive later that day from her brother. Allowed one visitor every fortnight, Tim Sutherland was Alice's only surviving relative and only visitor, rarely missing the first and third Sunday of each month; illness and infrequent overseas business trips being the only reasons he'd ever missed his date. He lived barely ten minutes' drive from the hospital, having bought a small cottage in the area some years ago.

Tim was not only Alice's big brother; he was "her life" as he'd constantly reminded her since her early years, when both parents had passed away within weeks of each other. Cancer in July and suicide September. Twenty-one-year-old Tim had taken responsibility for sorting out the family affairs, which included schooling eleven-year-old Alice and scraping an existence as an article clerk at Taylor & Woodbridge. Alice stopped rocking and slowly came back down to earth and the reality of her existence.

"Tim," she said. "Tim."

Eventually, the cornflakes and apple were eaten and the empty milk carton left in the bowl with the apple core and egg. Alice never ate the egg. She put on her slippers and dressing gown, which was fastened down the front by short lengths of shoelace, the original rope of the robe having been removed as a precautionary measure by her brother, in strict accordance with the official declaration he'd been required to sign as a registered visitor.

Seconds turned to minutes and eventually hours, during which time Alice combed her hair in front of the mirror, which was set in a metal frame and firmly bolted to the wall above the sink. Her hair was shoulder length and streaked with more grey than brown than should be on the head of a woman in her early forties. It was thin on top, where her scalp was clearly visible, and although the nurses had suggested she brush it less, the long, endless strokes of the brush seemed to have a calming effect on her tormented mind.

Alice placed her brush on the basin between the cold tap and where the hot tap should be, as her door opened once more. It was time for her to take the short walk to the ablutions, where a nurse would watch her undress and shower by herself, under one of the ten shower roses that stood in line over the long, ceramic-tiled wash trough. Large blocks of amber Lifebuoy soap were housed in recessed ceramic soap holders … soap for the body and hair applied and rinsed off in the allotted two-minute stay, under the unflinching gaze of the nurse. It was always the same nurse who escorted her to the showers and who took perverse pleasure from advising her which "bits" to do next and not to forget "to wash there". The same nurse who had held her legs down while she and three others forced Alice to take a lukewarm bath. That was the last time she had resisted a bath. One of them had dunked her head repeatedly under the water, cutting an eyelid with a fingernail or ring; one had punched her in the face a couple of times, breaking her nose in the process; and one had released her pinching grip on the thighs, taking advantage of the melee to thrust two or more fingers hard and deep inside the helpless inmate. Tepid baths were not for hygiene purposes, but forms of punishment administered for petty misdemeanours. There was a correlation between the severity of the crime and the temperature of the bath water. An ice-cold bath at six o'clock on a winter's morning was far more feared than a hiding with the buckle end of a nurse's belt.

Dressed in her green cotton tracksuit and slippers, Alice crumpled her towel and deposited it in the big wicker linen basket by the door and allowed herself to be escorted back to her room.

Inmate and minder passed half a dozen other inmates in the lounge. Two sat in front of a black-and-white television set, which was showing a gardening programme, though neither appeared to be watching the screen. Another played with a pack of cards at the large oak dining table. The cards were lined up in precise rows of six by four … all face down and serving no purpose. Alice shuffled back to her room and sat on the bed.

"Expecting a visitor today then, Alice?" said the nurse, just hinting at the possibility that this privilege may be withdrawn on a whim should she not tow the line.

"Tim."

"Tim." Repeated the nurse. "That's right, Alice. Be a good girl now and none of your nonsense."

"Nonsense" had come in the form of a bitten-off ear lobe and badly gouged eye three weeks ago. The recipient, a skinny mousey man with long straggly hair had taunted Alice in the garden and tried to grab her crotch from behind. She'd turned like a wounded tiger and savaged him with such ferocity that his face had required extensive treatment for the several bite wounds and scratch marks. He'd been lucky not to lose and eye and she'd been fortunate to receive the fairly minor punishment of single-cell confinement. She missed her garden with its beautifully manicured rolling lawns, winding cobbled pathways and beds of hollyhocks and rhododendron.

Tim would be here later, though she never knew what time of the day he would appear. Tim did things in his own time, he always had. "Wait for me, Alice, I've told you before," he used say, as he placed her meal, before her when she got home from school. "Don't do that, Alice … or you know what will happen."

Alice knew; and with time, she knew not to do that, or when to do that … and how he liked her to "do that" when he told her.

He'd told her what to say at the trial. Hadn't he always known what was best for her? Then later on he'd told her to say nothing at the trial. If only she'd listened to him, she wouldn't have screwed everything up for him … by getting pregnant. Not once, but then again. Tim knew who was responsible for James and he'd sorted it out his way. He'd waited for him outside the Pig & Whistle that Saturday night and then given him such a beating that the unfortunate fellow had spent eight weeks recovering in hospital from a cracked skull, broken jaw and fractured arm. Tim had used his cricket bat and even through chipped and jagged teeth, the victim was reluctant to give a name. No file was opened by the police, but the word was about that you "don't mess with Sutherland's sister" and nobody else did.

The Jaguar XJS pulled up as silently as was possible, given that the driveway to Rampton was constructed of coarse aggregate chips. Visitors' bays were demarcated by T-shaped signs embedded in front of the lavender hedge. There were five such signs, but each were ignored by the owner of the Jag, as they were not deemed close enough to the entrance for Tim Sutherland's comfort. He took a small package the size of a shoe box from the front passenger seat and locked the car. He crunched his brightly polished brown brogues the five or six paces across the gravel, to the small flight of grey granite entrance steps. A slight deviation to his right told him that the snail shell on the third step was occupied. He wiped the gooey remnants of the creature from the sole of his shoe on the next step and continued his march.

Although approaching his mid-fifties, Tim Sutherland cut a good-looking figure, six foot three, slim, but well defined and immaculately dressed in beige flannels, olive-green waistcoat and sports jacket. His hair was thick and an even silver throughout ... styled by Mario; he'd often been likened to Gregory Peck. Brown Revo sunglasses hung from his breast pocket and he exuded all the confidence of a self-made man.

The woman at reception had noticed him before. She was young enough to be his daughter, but old enough to want to hold his gaze just that little bit longer than one should, as he flirted with his dark blue eyes.

She thanked him for signing in. He said it was his pleasure and she told him that no, it was hers. A nurse was summoned to escort Mr Sutherland and as he waited he flirted a little more. Yes, that was his Jag outside and he'd love to take her for a spin one day ...

just so long as she'd agree to him buying her lunch, or dinner. He thought about adding breakfast as a postscript, but was glad he didn't as the line was tacky and would have coincided with the arrival of a burly woman escort, who looked every bit the opposite of the pert little brunette he'd been chatting to.

"You forgot this," said the young girl, pointing to the brown package she was holding out for him.

"What would I do without you?" said Tim, offering a hint of a wink and receiving a hint of a smile in exchange.

Alice's door was unlocked by the chubby, rough hands of the escort, who'd shared not one word with her male companion during their five-minute walk along corridors and across courtyards. He entered the room and the door was closed, but not locked behind him.

"Hello, Alice," said Tim. "How are you doing, then?" His sister was sitting on the edge of the bed, staring ahead at the basin on the opposite side of the room. She said nothing, nor did she acknowledge his presence. Her brother walked slowly towards her with measured steps. He wiped the unpainted iron raised railing that was the foot of the bed with his index finger and almost immediately brushed imaginary dust from the palms of his hands before removing his jacket and carefully folding it over the offending rail. The package was carefully placed at the foot of the bed.

Tim approached Alice and stood with his legs apart and as close as he could to his sister, without their bodies actually touching. Without warning, he raised his right arm, gripping his sister's jaw, digging fingers and thumb deep into her cheeks … prizing apart her mouth and simultaneously jerking her face towards his. His fingers and thumb were inches apart as they met with no resistance. Alice's lips were pursed and her mouth was open and gaped like that of a landed and stranded cod.

His voice was controlled and calm, but purposeful and chilling.

"I said hello, Alice … how … are … you … doing?" he whispered into her face, his breath mingling with her own, as their lips almost met in an incestuous kiss. She could not reply, as his grip had tightened just ever so little by little, as each word was uttered. She mumbled some inaudible words by way of an answer and the vice that locked her jaw was eased by a notch or two.

"I'm okay, Tim, I'm fine … I'm fine, Tim. Thank you."

"That's better, Alice," said Tim, lifting his sister up off the bed, but gently and with cupped hands under her aching jowls. "You know I know what's best for you, don't you? Of course you do, Alice. Always have."

Tim walked around the room with his hands behind his back, as if inspecting the Royal household. His walk was always the same; slow, upright, dignified. A stranger may pass him off as an ex-military man, such was his gait and demeanour. His little tour ended where it had started and he placed his hands on Alice's shoulders pressing her down to sit on the edge of the bed again, just where he wanted her. He'd always had her just where he wanted her.

"Don't you want to know what I've brought you, Alice?" She nodded, which was answer enough.

"I don't suppose you remember that it's your birthday on Tuesday, do you?" he continued. "Anyway, I've got this for you," he said, wafting the present in front of her eyes. "But first of all we must have our little chat again. You do remember our little chats?"

"Yes, Tim," replied the woman in front of him, her hands scratching her thighs through tracksuit pants. Backwards and forwards at an ever-increasing pace and intensity, scratching and rocking … scratch, scratch, with eagles' talons, digging fingers deep into her own cotton-covered flesh.

Tim stood in front of his sister once more. He placed the palms of his hands over her face covering her eyes. He slid them gently up towards her brow, running his perfectly manicured fingers back through her still damp hair. Three or four strokes of her hair tightened her body rigid. He gripped the hair at the back of her head and pulled her towards his groin.

"You do remember what you did all those years ago, don't you, Alice?" She could barely breathe from the side of her mouth, but managed a "Yes, Tim". She repeated the words, as he tugged her closer.

"Say it, Alice. Say it for me again. You know what I like to hear," Tim said, pulling tighter and thrusting his pelvis forward and deeper into her face.

"It was me, Tim ... I did it … it was me."

"Good girl, Alice," said Tim, somewhat grateful, almost relieved. "Good girl. Now open your present."

He placed the package on her lap and helped her unwrap the brown post office paper. She tore off the final piece, to reveal a twelve-inch doll dressed in a Laura Ashley baby outfit. The face of the baby was porcelain, a collector's piece of intricate detail, painted by hand and almost real in every facial feature.

"Emily," said Alice, clutching the doll to her breast.

"Yes, Emily," replied Tim. "Your little Emily."

Tim stooped down and lifted his sister's chin with his bent forefinger, kissing her gently on her lips. "Your little Emily" he continued.

Tim tugged ever so lightly at the doll and felt the resistance as Alice held fast.

"Alice!" said Tim and her grip was relinquished.

Tim took the doll and held it dangling by one leg, close to his side. "Alice," he repeated, beckoning her to look up, as he retreated towards her sink.

"You know what happens when you don't do what I want you to, don't you?" Tim said, holding the doll high above his head. He nodded, just to emphasise his point.

The porcelain face broke into a dozen pieces as it met the corner of the porcelain basin, sending shards of cheek, nose and forehead to all parts of the room. The faceless baby was dropped to the floor and finished off with the heel of a brogue like a half-lit fag end on a cold concrete pavement.

"Happy birthday, Alice," Tim whispered as he picked up his jacket and headed for the door. "Now be a good girl, won't you."

The door shut behind the man in his flannel, brogues and jacket. He fired a broad smile towards the girl at reception and she winked her response. Her took a tissue from his pocket and wiped some dust from his shoe, before switching on the ignition of the Jag and gliding back down the gravel road.

"Alice! What on earth did you do that for?" shouted the nurse, as her flat-soled shoes cracked a jagged piece of porcelain underfoot.

"You're heading for a cold bath if you carry on like this, my girl."

FLYING KITES

Rain lashed the office window with such force and intensity that Hugh Stuart thought the glass may well give way as it rattled and creaked before the unrelenting gale that had gripped southern England for the past couple of days. At least he had a window, unlike many of his colleagues at the firm of Waterson, Prescott & Chambers. That's what you got after twenty five years with WPC: a work station with a window, a cocktail party in your honour and a handshake from the chairman.

Condensation formed easily on the glass, helped by the constant recommended optimum working temperature of his office. Hugh neither knew, nor cared what that may be. It was however, uncomfortably warm and he loosened his tie, stretching over his work station keyboard towards the window. He placed two fingers as high up the glass as he could reach and ran them an inch or two down the pane. Little droplets formed immediately and eagerly began their zigzag race to the sill. Hugh bet that the righthand droplet would win. He lost. He and his sister had played that game in their mother's kitchen almost forty years ago. It brought back vivid memories, as clear as the small blue patch of sky breaking through the black clouds in the distance.

That small patch of blue grew larger and allowed the sun to stream through the glass, filling the office with a strange amber glow as the rain continued to tap dance on the window. It was June and it was supposed to be summer. This was without doubt the wettest, bleakest summer he could recall. What had happened to the summers of past years? Were they as glorious as he remembered, or did the passing of time simply play tricks on the mind?

Hugh swung his chair towards the window, lifted his head slightly and closed his eyes to the warm glare of the sun. It was the summer of 1966 again and he remembered it so vividly that he could almost reach out and grasp it with both hands. He could smell the fresh-cut grass and taste the vanilla ice cream, licked from sticky little fingers, as it ran down the sides of a soggy cone. The white noise of the office became the distant lapping of the incoming tide on the rounded pebbles of Whitstable beach. Granny Stuart's hut was the bright red one and third from the end. Yellow, blue, Granny's hut, another blue one, a couple of greens and so on, all busy with action as families descended on their chalets for a day at the seaside.

Young Hugh picked at a piece of flaking red paint, easing it from the rounded timber handrail that guarded the single flight of stairs to the chalet. Irresistible to a ten-year-old, flaky paint picking was almost as enjoyable as teasing the hell out of a little sister.

Granny, Mum, two sisters, Aunty Pat and Cousin Kathryn were all in the chalet making cucumber-and-egg sandwiches and pouring hot water from the thermos flask into the teapot.

Hugh had been chased from the chalet for twice raiding the biscuit tin and now he was sulking at the bottom of the stairs, picking paint and licking the tips of his fingers for the last remnants of the milk chocolate, that had once coated digestive biscuits. Dad was playing cricket away that Saturday and was reluctant to take his son to Dartford. Hugh hadn't really wanted to go to the beach. With nobody to play with and nothing to do, he was bored.

The yellow hut had some older boys, but he didn't want to ask them to play. They were busy in a game of cricket with their father on the narrow strip of cracked concrete promenade that separated the chalets from beach. Hugh decided that they weren't very good, as one boy was clearly throwing instead of bowling, whilst the other was fetching everything from wide outside where his off stump would be. As a result, their tennis ball ended up on the beach more often than not, causing a prolonged break in their game, whilst the grown-up ball retriever ran down the concrete stairs and onto the beach.

Hugh hung around the yellow hut, because although their standard of cricket wasn't the best, they had their radio tuned into the test match at Trent Bridge. The West Indies had dismissed

England cheaply and were now battling. They were off to a decent start … and they had Sobers!

Hugh sprung to his feet and skipped down the prom a short distance in the other direction, away from the huts. He had fingers down the seam and slightly off-line, as he commentated quietly to himself … "John Snow in to Kanhai."

He started on his long run-up, swerved around an old lady walking her poodle and delivered his imaginary bouncer to Kanhai, who ducked well inside the line, hooking the delivery one-handed down to fine leg for four. Snow walked back to his mark, but in the same direction away from the huts and moments later was steaming in again to the great West Indian batsman.

Three deliveries into the over and Snow's mother cried out for him to come and get some cake and orange squash, so the remainder of the over had to be bowled from "the other end" back into the breeze. Hugh reached the chalets at the same time as Mr Yellow Hut came panting up the steps from the beach, tennis ball in hand for the umpteenth time.

The family picnic was laid out on a tartan blanket that did little to soften the feel of the rounded stones that masqueraded as beach along most of the southeastern coastline. Timber breakwaters divided the beach into forty-yard stretches of unforgiving tar-covered pebble purgatory.

Hugh washed down three slices of his grandmother's jam sponge cake with a gallon of orange squash and tiptoed his way down to the water's edge for a short-lived swim. His mother called him over and he gingerly picked his way back up the beach and sat down beside her. She wrapped him up in a large beach towel and rubbed his hair dry vigorously, in that motherly way that mothers do so annoyingly. She had a surprise for the young boy, but first she had to scrape a large dollop of tar from between his toes with a lollipop stick.

Hugh's mother had been up to the chalet and reappeared with a paper shopping bag, from which she now produced some brightly coloured fabric, two bamboo sticks and a ball of string. Within minutes and with a little intuition, they had the kite assembled on the rug and ready to go. The kite was a back-up plan for the young boy, only to be used in case of emergency and freshening wind. The conditions were perfect and, with the aid of the latest edition of the Gravesend Reporter, half a dozen newspaper tails were tied to a length of string at the end of the kite.

Hugh ran up the steps to the promenade and from there up another short flight of timber steps to the wide expanse of grass that was a feature of Whitstable's seafront. The kite was laid on the grass and Hugh paced out yards of string into the wind. His first run succeeded in getting the kite a few feet off the ground, before it went into a suicidal death roll and plummeted head first into the ground. Another two failed attempts before Hugh felt the strain of the string as his kite soared into the cloudless sky and out over the chalets in the distance.

Hugh squinted as the kite cut a path across the sun and for a fleeting moment he held it there, a blazing fireball glowing through the red-and-green patches of cotton and bamboo crucifix high above. A seagull entered from the west and mocked the kite, holding still and transfixed against the forces of nature with effortless ease. The kite ducked and weaved to Hugh's command, newspaper telltales dancing their giddy way through the air, as a cobra to a master charmer's tune. The young boy had complete control of his flying machine, which obeyed his every command. He turned his back and pulled the string from over his shoulder. He skipped and danced and spun around, swapping hands to keep control.

A green litter bin stood sentry duty in the middle of the vast expanse of grass, just feet away from the boy. He had the string in his right hand and over his shoulder. It was Derek Underwood now to Kanhai, as Hugh began his run-up, left arm around the bin. Kanhai was done in the flight by one, which skidded through the slightest of gaps between bat and pad. As Hugh jumped for joy, the kite stalled and faltered a little.

Underwood walked slowly back to his mark, rolling up the sleeve of his left arm, whilst skilfully holding onto the kite strings.

His walk was flat-footed and ungainly, but his run in to bowl was as smooth and graceful as a ballerina. Hugh loved to watch Underwood bowl whenever Kent were at playing at Canterbury, or occasionally in Gravesend. He had Underwood's signature in a little red autograph book, along with Knott, Cowdrey and Mike Denness. A few more left-arm-around-bin deliveries had the Windies in all sorts of trouble. Underwood had picked up the wickets of Kanhai, Butcher and Nurse in quick succession, but the great Garfield Sobers was still there.

Hugh's interest in the kite waned, as it became increasingly difficult to control, whilst bowing to Sobers. The kite was landed and placed twenty paces from the bin. A short run from kite back to bin saw the last of Snow's deliveries for the day.

Underwood continued to bowl away from the bin end for the most part of the afternoon. Passers-by stopped to watch the young boy, as over after over went by without a break, little leaps and skips accompanied by frantic but unsuccessful appeals. At one point, a poodle relieved himself on the kite, as Underwood waddled back to his mark, oblivious to the canine's pitch invasion. Hugh's mother joined the small crowd of onlookers when she walked up the stairs in search of her son, whose kite no longer flew above their beach.

"Howzat?" Underwood implored, as loudly as his little voice could shout. Charlie Elliot slowly raised his finger and Sobers was gone! Hugh ran in circles, arms outstretched to his side in unbridled joy. Holford, then Hendricks and he'd be into the tail.

The sun was setting low in the sky and families were packing up and locking up chalets for another day. Picnic baskets and blankets were stacked with deck chairs at the bottom of the stairs that led to the cricket ground above, where the young blond English debutant had single-handedly given his team a great chance of going 2 – 1 up in the series.

The Stuarts packed their belongings into the boot of their Humber Hawk, waved goodbye to Cousin Kathryn and Aunty Pat and began their short journey home. Hugh contemplated his six-wicket haul, whilst miles away in Nottingham, Derek Underwood sat in his dressing room contemplating his first test match. Two overs for none in the first innings and no wickets yet in the second. His deadly days were yet to come.

"Get you a coffee, Hugh?" came the voice from behind the shoulder-high office partition. Hugh was immediately transported several decades forward to the present.

"What? Um … yes. Thanks."

He gazed out the window. The storm was over and clouds dispatched elsewhere. The sun shone brightly and high above a large oak tree, as a seagull entered from the west, holding still and transfixed against the forces of nature with effortless ease.

THE SHORT STORY

Four years, three manuscripts, two near offers and one very determined writer later saw Martin James Donald typing away as usual at his laptop, woollen beanie to cover his bald spot and reading glasses perched precariously on the end of his nose. His sweater was the one his mother had knitted and given him for Christmas years before. The same one he changed into every evening, after dinner and before he sat at his desk. It was his lucky sweater, complete with Santa and Rudolph ... well, one day it would be his lucky sweater; and then all his hours of toil and rejection would have been worthwhile.

Martin rented a small one-bedroom, semi-detached townhouse in a secure gated complex in the Cape Town suburb of Wynberg. He'd been there for just over three years, having been unable to cope with the gardening and shear size of his late mother's house, which he'd inherited upon her death. With no siblings to share her estate, Martin had tried to maintain the house as best he could. He finally sold it for less than its worth, in favour of renting a small place of his own. With a concrete garden and local maintenance man to call upon if needed, he was free to concentrate on his nine-to-four bank job and passion for writing.

His cream woolly sweater left only the collar of his fully buttoned formal shirt protruding and the poly-cotton permanent-press brown trousers did nothing to suggest that Martin ever got dressed with the lights on. Black brogue shoes and orange socks completed his attire. He had never been one to worry about such things, not even thirty-five years ago when he attended Wynberg Boys' High School had he been able to "look the part", which was a mighty difficult achievement, considering their strictly enforced dress code. Even in uniform, Martin made an easy target for prefects and teachers alike, whether it be odd socks (both grey, but one inside out), dusty blazer, stained shorts.

At fifty-three years old, Martin cut a sorry figure at the bank and, despite having achieved promotion though longevity, was not a popular choice of assistant bank manager, being incapable of management and introverted in the extreme. His loathing of confrontation had often found him locked in a toilet cubicle for the entire duration of a scheduled staff meeting. Several staff, whenever nature called, would delight in publically announcing to the world that they were "off to do a Martin", amid stifled chuckles and suppressed sniggers.

For Martin Donald, the only encouragement he had ever received for anything he did was from his doting mother. From his earliest days, right up until her death, Martin's mother had called him either "Smartin" or "Smarty Marty", even on the few occasions that classmates had attended early birthday parties. As fewer friends replied to his invitations, or accepted only to have 'flu when his big day arrived, he gradually declined his mother's suggestion to have a "birthday bash", preferring to celebrate alone with his mother. Twelve, thirteen and fourteen - candle birthday cakes were all enjoyed by mother and son, as were all subsequent cakes through to his forty-ninth cake.

He grew up not knowing his father, other than that he had been a captain in the army, was very handsome and had run off with some woman when Martin was a few months old, leaving all his possessions behind, including his wife and son. Wardrobes of clothing and chests full of belongings remained locked away for years, awaiting his return. Those very same wardrobes and chests had been sorted through by Martin and all but a few items sold off on his behalf by the executors of the will. His mother's side of the family had sufficient inherent wealth to ensure that life was not a struggle, in the fatherless household.

When his mother was buried, the fifty-year-old assistant bank manager withdrew even further into his little world of office walls by day and townhouse walls by night. He walked to work and home again; ten minutes there and fifteen minutes back. Ham, cheese and tomato rolls for lunch and spaghetti bolognaise at night. Sometimes dinner would vary a bit, with perhaps a helping of shepherd's pie, macaroni or lasagne. It was the dinner that

71

accounted for the extra time it took Martin to walk home, as the evening meal was always one bought from the garage filling-station shop and one that required the removal of cardboard, then tin foil and finally four minutes in the microwave. Cardboard, newspapers and two-litre plastic Coke bottles accounted for his weekly recycle garbage bag.

Encouraged by his late mother's ascertain that "Smartin, you really should have stuck with your English, you know, when you left Wynberg," Martin had enrolled on a Creative Writing correspondence course and thereafter commenced his first novel. It wasn't going to take him too long. He didn't have a television to distract him and, apart from work, reading a novel a month and cooking supper every evening, he had plenty of time to devote to his new hobby. Maybe it would become more than a hobby; maybe he would be required to attend book signings, where fellow employees from the bank would queue for hours just to get a personal scribble in their copy of his latest best seller thriller... The Bank by Martin Donald.

"Not taking long" took nearly eighteen months. Google had told him that sixty-five-thousand words would be enough to consider it a Novel and he'd also acquired a long list of potential publishers by the same means. In fact, Martin had come to depend on his internet browsing, constantly checking his "either" or "neither", "which" or "what" and "past" or "passed."

For the first time in his life, Martin was proud of himself, truly proud. If only his mother were there to read his finished product. It was by no means autobiographical, despite the mysterious murder taking place in a bank not dissimilar to his own. He wasn't sure what thoughts or subliminal forces drew him in that direction, but the more he wrote, the easier it got and the clearer the path forward to completion.

As Martin typed "The End" and pressed "Print", he looked down at the pile of printed copies next to his desk. It was two o'clock in the morning, but he had finished. He rolled his head and felt a grinding click in the back of his neck, as vertebrae reminded him that they needed a rest. Seven revisions of his manuscript lay on the floor, each with countless notes, comments and corrections in scribbled red Biro. The walls of his lounge were painted cream and a single pair of "one-size-fits-all" green curtains shut out the world.

Martin stared at one blank wall and imagined he would soon be needing to erect a shelf, one with solid book ends and sturdy enough to take the load of five or six best-sellers. "Another blockbuster from the pen of Mr Donald." He smiled to himself, eyelids heavy with sleep. "Possibly the best read of the year - The Times." As he dragged himself upstairs to bed, his last thoughts that night were of whether to publish under the name of Martin

Donald, or M.J. Donald. It had worked for A.A., H.G. and of course J.K., so why shouldn't it work as well for M.J.?

Luckily, the next day was Saturday and not the one in three he was required to work. Martin was up early, showered and finished with breakfast of corn flakes and coffee, all before eight o'clock. He had a busy day ahead. Today was the first day in life of M.J. Donald, multimillion-copy-selling author, frequent talkshow guest and Oscar nominated for his Best Adapted Screenplay.

He had a list of potential publishers and literary agents to go through, most of which he'd tagged for easy access in the weeks leading up to this day. He was familiar with their requirements, most insisting on a cover letter, brief synopsis and the first two or three chapters, depending on length of copy. Some requested a brief author biography and details of previously published material, if any.

Well read on the do's and don'ts of manuscript submission, Martin chose to ignore those who would have him approaching only a few agents and publishers at a time ... "Remember, many agents deal with a multitude of publishers, so don't play all your cards at once." By Sunday evening, Martin had neatly filed away on his laptop cover letters to fifty-three agents and publishers in South Africa, the U.K. and United States. He had even penned a few letters to agents in Australia and Canada, but decided to hold them back, somewhat belatedly heeding the advice not to flood the market.

Monday in the bank took an eternity to pass. The ham rolls were finished before noon and the afternoon dragged by interminably. The second hand on Martin's office clock was taking pleasure from his pain, increasing in volume but completing each revolution in ever-slower time. Was the tick louder than the tock and why wasn't the minute hand moving? Was it two o'clock … five past two.? Five? He wondered if he would have more than five requests to see his complete manuscript when he got home. If he'd sent them from work, he would know by now; but he hadn't and, anyway, that would be asking for trouble … assistant manager or not.

Even the walk home seemed to take longer. Martin fumbled for his keys, pushing his shoulder to the front door even before it was properly unlocked. His shopping bag of cannelloni, Coke and paper were flung onto the kitchen table and he paced to the lounge and his laptop, left open and plugged, where it had been since the night before. As his computer started up, he noticed the memory stick back-up lying next to the laptop. He tutted to himself and made a mental note to keep a back-up in his office at all times in future.

"Send/receive" came and went. He had two messages, neither of which revealed the subject matter. One told him that he had just won a million dollars in a lottery he hadn't even entered, the other was from a cell phone network offering him the chance to obtain a free phone. Martin quickly pressed "send/receive" once more, then deleted the two spam messages. He stared blankly at his screen, unable to comprehend that he hadn't received any replies to his manuscript submissions. That day at the office, he had told one co-worker of his imminent publishing contract. The sceptical associate relayed the news and before long the subject matter of tea room gossip and giggles was "Martin's bestseller".

Martin had read the publishers' web pages, which told him not to expect a reply within eight to ten weeks and not to contact them in the interim, but he'd thought that his submission would be the exception to the rule.

Several weeks passed and Martin grew more and more despondent. His first reply had come almost a week after he had embarked on his mission to be published and now nearly three weeks later, he had received two confirmations of receipt and three very curt "thanks but no thanks" replies, without so much as an explanation.

Work was becoming intolerable, even more so than before. It was as if the staff were all jackals and he a wounded buck. One by one they would sniff him out and close in for a bite, tearing lumps of flesh as they sank their drooling jaws into him.

"Written any bestsellers today, Martin?"

"How's that book publishing contract coming along, then?"

The assistant bank manager would invariably retreat to the toilets or the privacy of his own office, despite his more senior position in the office. The buck was much bigger than the jackal and look how that one panned out.

The three weeks turned into three months, then four and five. Christmas came and went, which meant that it had been eight months and all he had to show for it was a handful of rejection e-mails. By now, it was a familiar tune to his ears.

"Hi, Martin. Thank you for your manuscript submission. Unfortunately it is not suitable for our target market." Although he retrieved some of his unanswered e-mail submissions and followed up with very polite reminders, those that failed to initially respond seldom did so after being reminded.

As more and more time passed, replies trickled in, but none offered the faintest hope of publication; the only exceptions being the so-called "vanity" publishing offers, which usually went to great lengths to explain how they were not "vanity" publishers, but "for a contribution" towards publishing costs, would have your book printed, bound, distributed and on the shelves, before you could say "Stephen King". Martin's research had been thorough and he wasn't about to let vanity get the upper hand and allow himself to be snared by their traps.

The fifteen-minute walk home was now a routine ten minutes, as the one-shop, quick-stop was foregone in his eagerness to get home and review his correspondence. The weekly shop now entailed doubling up on bread, ham, cheese, tomatoes and Coke, which became Martin's staple diet. Often, the sheer disappointment of receiving no replies would leave Martin feeling tired, dejected and incapable of even preparing his evening sandwich and Coke.

Martin's attempt to cast his net further afield and send manuscripts to potential publishers in the United States resulted in a multitude of self-publishing offers and an increased amount of spam mail, as suggestions and offers were received from unknown agents, publishers and spin-off companies.

At work, all talk of bestsellers and publishers was very much initiated by co-workers. Martin had ceased to mention the subject months ago; indeed he was mentioning less and less, as time went by. Seldom seen, other than fleeting glimpses between his office and the toilets, his job credentials were being questioned by many in the bank, including his superiors. One Monday morning, Martin was rebuked by the local area manager, who told him in no uncertain terms that if he continued on this path, there would be no option, but to issue a written warning. What was he doing all day, that he could let his work pile up, unattended?

Martin pretty much "Googled" his weekends and evenings away. If he wasn't searching for new literary agents or potential publishers, he was reading up on new correspondence courses, joining one that offered a course in short-story writing. They also ran a quarterly short story competition, which sounded quite appealing. He discovered a multitude of competitions worldwide, most of which required the entrant comply with stringent terms and conditions. Mainly in the two or three thousand word category, Martin discovered that Hemingway had once written a six-word short story! It read, "Baby shoes for sale: never worn." Martin thought it pretty inspiring, but doubted if the author would have been required to submit the obligatory first couple of words, cover letter and synopsis.

Undaunted, Martin penned his first short story, followed two days later by another. The themes of these were similar, if not identical, and were lifted from select passages of his unpublished novel. Cut, paste, edit, print, edit and so it continued. Both short stories were entitled "The Bank" and each complied with their respective competition word-count restrictions. Martin was pleased with his shorter version, but delighted with the final 2 956-word version of "The Bank", which he duly saved in the original word.doc format and then again in the .pdf version, required by at least six currently running competitions.

The completed short stories were then backed up on a memory stick. Martin put his hands behind his head and rocked back on the feet of his chair. He nodded with satisfaction, a smirk revealing a small dimple on the left side of his otherwise, emotionless face. Martin immediately opened the file containing his seventy-thousand word novel and sent it directly to his recycle bin. The smirk disappeared, only to be replaced by a sneer, as Martin picked up a full glass of Coke and hurled it at the bare, shelfless wall. He sat and watched the outer remnants of the brown sticky liquid trickle down the paintwork.

In total, eight competitions were entered. Five of the shorter versions and three of the other were e-mailed to their respective destinations and the completion fee was paid on line, usually being in the region of 5 euro or 7 pounds. It was early April and initial postings of the shortlisted manuscripts would appear before the end of June. One magazine in Ireland would not longlist or even shortlist potential winners. They would announce the first three prize winners on 30 June. He adapted, edited, printed and saved to the appropriate format several versions of his story, which were then posted or e-mailed to various other global entities, along with the required competition entrance fee.

The next few weeks were excruciating. Martin went through the motions at work. He ignored his colleagues' jibes and the warning letter received from Head Office. He bypassed the quick shop, though there was no need to rush home. His only trip to the shops was on Saturday morning, or the next day if he was required to work at the weekend. Cheese rolls, Google, Coke and work... week after week.

With no sign of his name appearing in any of the posted lists that went out at the end of the month, Martin's rage simmered within. He ran out of crockery to throw at the wall, but would constantly stab at the desk with a breadknife, which became warped and bent, like the inner workings of his mind. The leather top became gouged and jagged, splintered pieces of oak projected through the green top like shards of glass.

Martin had long since lost count of the cover letters, competition entries and manuscripts submitted since his quest began.

On 7 July, Martin stood up from his desk, stepped over the broken plates, empty Coke tins and newspapers that littered his floor. His laptop stood open on the once beautiful desk that had been part of his inheritance. The screen was on and e-mail open, but nothing had entered the "inbox" for two days. It was mid-morning and Martin was late for work, a couple of hours late. His phone had rung unanswered and was ringing once more as he opened a chest of drawers next to his front door. On the top shelf was a small children's case of brown leather, with two simple locks, but no key necessary. Martin sprung open the locks and removed a shoe box of his mother's photos, some lace handkerchiefs and a silver cigarette box. The purpose of his search was then carefully lifted from the case – a revolver and box containing fourteen rounds of ammunition. He loaded six bullets, retained the remainder in the box and, holding the weapon in his right hand, left his apartment. With his left hand he slammed the door closed behind him.

The walk to the bank took the usual ten minutes. Martin entered as would any member of the public via a set of security doors. Between the doors, the small indicator in front of him flashed bright green and released the second door. He removed his left hand from his jacket pocket and pushed open the door. The bank had several customers that morning, either scribbling in cubicles or waiting patiently in the single-line service queue. Tellers were about their business, as Martin walked unnoticed to the security door, which separated staff from the public. His right hand remained in his pocket as his left punched in the six-digit security code that would allow him access.

At home, Martin's laptop received a message from a magazine in Ireland. Attached was a letter, which would later be read by the first investigating officer to visit Martin's apartment.

Dear Mr Donald,

May we offer our congratulations upon your short story submission entitled "The Bank" being awarded first prize by our panel of judges. Your story will appear in our year-end short story anthology and you will receive 5000 euros prize money as advertised.

We would also like to take this opportunity to apologise for the delay in announcing the prize-winning submission, but such was the interest in this prestigious award that the unusual decision was taken by the judges to extend the adjudication process.

We look forward to receiving more from the desk of M.J. Donald and, if I may quote one of our judges, "This writer shows great insight into the complexities of a disturbed mind. His ability to transfer that knowledge to the printed word is a rare talent and one that should be fostered and nurtured. I'm sure we will all be hearing a great deal more from the pen of Mr Donald."

Regards,

The Editor

NETS

The mower was returned to the shed that once served as a storage facility for the small dairy farm on the rural outskirts of Cape Town. Animal feed, a tractor, trailer and various other pieces of farming plant and machinery were once housed in the timber-framed building that was now home to a tractor, trailer and various other pieces of sporting plant and machinery.

The Farm had been carved up like a Sunday roast by the previous owner over a decade ago and a sizeable portion donated to the local community for recreational use as a sports ground. Two rugby fields guarded a cricket square in the middle of "The Rec", as locals referred to it, and a functional rectangular face-brick clubhouse kept the shed company at night. The burglar bars on every window and door kept it secure.

Arthur Sutton was the man who had returned the mower. It was early September and the rugby posts were back in the shed along with the rusty old steel-framed terraced timber spectators' stand, neither of which would see the light of day for seven more months. He had prepared the cricket pitch for a friendly game that coming weekend. It would probably be a lively wicket so early in the season, but he'd taken as much grass off it as he dare and given it a good, heavy rolling during a lucky break in the recent wet weather. The same again on Friday and there shouldn't be too many complaints, come the weekend. The outfield was looking good after this morning's haircut and all that remained for him to do was a little white lining and those bloody cricket nets. God, how he hated those bloody nets.

The task of converting "The Rec" from one seasonal sporting facility to another wasn't a particularly onerous one. Twice a year Arthur would have a little too much on his plate, but players and well-meaning locals would invariably help him out, eager to get their respective seasons off to the best of starts. Help had been required to wheel the heavy cages of the cricket nets back into position, just off the twenty-two-metre line of the rugby pitch furthest from the clubhouse. Somehow, though, there never seemed to help around to fix the netting to the cages.

Arthur sat on the light roller, just inside the giant double doors of the shed. Next to him was a large Oregon pine chest which, were it not for the three layers of green paint, would have been considered a valuable piece of furniture, worthy of the best of Constantia residences. Nobody had bothered to scratch the surface of the chest and, as such, it housed the groundkeeper's paints, thinners and paint brushes. Arthur unlocked the chest with the aid of a huge bunch of keys he wore at all times from his belt. He held the lid open and stared at the half-dozen tins of paint. Removing an unopened bottle of Klipdrift brandy, he let gravity close the chest lid for him. When he returned the bottle ten minutes later, it was two thirds empty … but one third fuller than his life.

The tray of the three-wheeled white lining machine was filled with five litres of lining paint and slowly pushed out of the shed. Arthur followed the path of the boundary rope he had set out earlier that day, opening the little sluice gate behind the front wheel; he kept the rear left wheel tight against the rope and completed one circuit of the outfield. He closed the sluice gate and returned to his seat on the roller, pouring the remainder of the paint back into the tin and the remainder of the brandy down his throat. He had three more bottles in reserve, so he should be fine for the next couple of days.

It was nearly midday and a break in the cloud cover let a beam of bright sunlight cut through the slender vertical gap between the open shed door and frame. It cut a laser beam path across Arthur's shoes and off past the tractor tyre and beyond. If he didn't erect the cricket nets, he'd have to do it another time, as it was expected they would be ready before the first game of the season. The playing surface of the nets practice area had been prepared and was looking good. The cages were in place thanks to Martin, Sean and Piet from the first team, so there was no excuse.

Tall, somewhat malnourished through neglect and with a full head of spiky grey hair, Arthur was more than capable of erecting the nets by himself. They were already loaded on the trailer, as was the step ladder required to fasten the netting to the top horizontal members of the cages. There were four cages in all that needed netting and, luckily for Arthur, the ceiling of each net was a permanent wire fixture extending about three metres from one end – for that unwanted flying top edge.

The fifty-eight-year-old groundsman halted the tractor and trailer next to the line of cages, but remained seated. He took a tin of self-rolled cigarettes from his left breast pocket and a box of matches from the other. His teeth were irregular and nicotine stained, not having received dental care for nearly thirty years. Four teeth, including one front one, had long since departed. Arthur placed half a cigarette precariously between his lips, returning the other half to the tin and managed to run his open palm across his face, without dislodging it. His skin was rough and permanently sun baked, even in the winter months. The stubble on his face was grey and uneven. Occasionally, he would use an old discarded razor and soap from the changing-room dispenser to smarten up his appearance, but his beard was slow growing and patchy.

The cigarette was stubbed out on the inside of the trailer, where it joined a dozen or so similarly discarded butts. Arthur set the ladder, dragged the tangled web of olive-green netting from the trailer and began the annual ritual of separating the twelve individual pieces and laying them out on the grass. He always wondered how they could be carefully rolled up and stored at the end of the summer, only to be inexplicably tangled and twisted by the start of the next season.

As Arthur climbed the ladder and fixed the little steel hooks into the eyes welded onto the steel cages, the netting spread out before his eyes. It was always the same with these fucking nets. They brought back memories he'd managed to supress all these years. He never spoke of such things to anyone. In fact he never really spoke to anyone … about anything.

With the small amount he earned each week as groundsman, added to the two part-time gardening jobs he held down, Arthur scraped together just enough to rent a small room at a nearby riding stables, buy brandy, tobacco, bread, milk and biscuits. At weekends, he would eat the odd complimentary hotdog or cheese burger, courtesy of the sympathetic kitchen wives and girlfriends, who prepared players' meals and fast-food delights for a few hungry local and visiting spectators.

Arthur stood on the third rung of the ladder and gripped the green curtain of netting in front of his face with clenched, outstretched fists. He pulled it towards his body and pressed his stubbly face hard against the knots of the netting. The thin knotted rope played diamond-shaped pastry cutter on his cheeks the other side of the netting, as tears tricked from bloodshot eyes. It was as if the nets were some sort of mysterious dream catchers in his life. But these weren't dreams, nor were they nightmares. They were actual memories; a reality from which he could not hide. He thought he would run away and forget, but just when he least expected it, a little pink tricycle abandoned next to the club house would send him back thirty years, through a nauseating dark vortex of time travel, each horrendous visit eroding great chunks of sanity from his mind. The fucking cricket nets did that to him, as well. Many years ago, he'd tried to end the pain with rope, then months later pills and whisky were his choice. His ex-wife Mary had scoffed when told by friends of his various failed suicide attempts. "He can't even get that fucking right," she had said bitterly. It hadn't always been like that. Arthur gripped the net and rewound his memory tapes to a time before white lining, brandy and a living hell.

In 1982 Arthur and Mary Sutton lived in a detached house in the village of Clovelly, not far from the future sports grounds, which would have Arthur cutting, mowing and white lining thirty years later. Arthur played golf at the club they overlooked from their house, which they bought for a good price and renovated with love, turning it from house to home. Arthur was an associate with a leading architectural practice in Cape Town and had already been earmarked as a director before too long, despite his tender age. Mary taught English and Geography at the local high school. They had two young children, three budgies and a dog named Biscuit.

Arthur had completely redesigned their house, incorporating an extended garage, additional bedroom, entertainment deck and a small swimming pool, which due to the sloping terrain of their property, involved more engineering design work than the young architect had anticipated.

Mary woke early that Saturday morning and made tea for one, coffee for one and hot chocolate for two. The two chocolates were taken into the lounge where four-year-old Sandy was watching television with her twin brother Sammy. They had both been fed breakfast, as Mary had to go to go to school for a few hours that morning. It was the school play in less than six weeks and there were sets to be painted, costumes fashioned and lines rehearsed.

Arthur received his coffee in bed with a kiss and two slices of toast and marmalade. Mary showered, dressed, gave instructions to the children to be good and set off for school. It had blown a storm the night before, but the forecasters had done their job and correctly predicted a bright day ahead, with a light southeaster and a cloudless sunny day. The water in the newly completed swimming pool might be warm enough for a quick spring dip later that day. The children were constantly nagging him about going for a swim, so maybe today would be the day. For now, they seemed content to watch television and mess cookies on the carpet.

Having showered and changed into jeans and T-shirt, Arthur opened the sliding glazed aluminium doors onto the patio and filled his lungs. The overnight rain filled the cool morning air with the aroma of fynbos, but had also filled the pool with leaves and small twigs from an overhanging milkwood tree. If they were going to swim later, he would need to clean out the pool first.

The mandatory safety net had been stretched across the pool by the contractors just days before and fixed with small, bent stainless-steel hooks into purpose-made cleats embedded in the perimeter brick paving. True to form, the pool contractors hadn't quite fulfilled the obligations of their contract. The long-handled combination scoping net and scrubbing brush hadn't been delivered, so Arthur had bought a children's fishing net from Jimmy's Sports Shop nearby. It was a satisfactory enough piece of pool equipment, as a temporary measure. He unclipped just enough of the hooks to enable him to reach the leaves, which had congregated in the lea of the wind on the far side of the pool, and then proceeded back into the house to find his fishing net.

"Daddy, can I have a glass of milk please?" asked Sammy, tugging on his father's T-shirt as he stooped down low in search of the net at the back of a kitchen cupboard. Arthur abandoned his search and poured the boy a plastic tumbler of milk, leaving an inch or two in the bottom of the bottle. He escorted his son back into the lounge, wiping up the trail of milk drops with his socks, as he went. The sight of her brother with a tumbler of milk prompted little Sandy to ask her father for the same. She wasn't happy when he returned from the kitchen with a similar tumbler containing no more than a mouthful of milk. There was no more milk in the house.

Arthur donned his slippers, grabbed his car keys and headed for his car. He would be back in less than ten minutes with the milk and a newspaper, as the café was no more than a few hundred metres down the road. He would maintain later that it was probably no more than six minutes.

The sound of Biscuit barking greeted Arthur as he opened his car door. He didn't usually bark, unless there was someone walking too close to their house. Garbage men would usually do it, but they came on Mondays. Instinctively, he began to run towards the house. By the time his key had found the keyhole and opened the front door, he had dropped the milk. The newspaper was still in the car. He would never read that edition, or any newspaper – ever again. Biscuit's barking was unceasing and getting louder, as Arthur charged through the hallway and dining room, connecting with a coffee table in the process. The sight that faced him was the same one he revisited over and over again; at the inquest, in his dreams and through the cricket nets.

An insane, spine-chilling, involuntary scream erupted from his body, though he didn't recall making the sound whenever he relived the moment. Sandy was lying face down in the water, her upper body resting partly submerged on a rolled-back section of the green safety netting. Her brother was similarly positioned, but under the net and beneath his sister. The dog raced round and round the pool, relentlessly barking in a demented frenzy. Arthur plunged into the pool, pulling the tiny bodies towards the steps simultaneously, one in each hand. The next few minutes were blind panic. He recalled shouting "NO" several times and repeating the word over in his mind. Two tiny white bodies lay outstretched on the paving as their father shouted for help. He couldn't leave them and didn't know which he should revive, as both appeared beyond help. He frantically alternated between shouting for help and trying to breathe life into each child. Three for Sandy, three for Sammy, shout for help. Where the hell were the neighbours? He turned his son over, not remembering the basics of the first-aid lessons learned at school over a decade before. Should he expel the water from the lungs first or pump their chests to get the heart going? There was no sign of life at all. He broke off and ran to the telephone in the hallway. He dialled the only two numbers he could remember, but neither were answered. .

It was a neighbour, outside washing his car, who first heard the commotion and came upon the scene. He dialled the ambulance from his own home and then realised his wife could do the emergency calls, whilst he rushed back next door to help where he could. It seemed an eternity to Arthur and his neighbour and by the time the ambulance and police arrived, the two men were drained, both physically and emotionally.

The medics had administered the necessary treatment poolside, but had stopped after ten or fifteen minutes. Nevertheless, they took the two small children away in the ambulance, lights flashing and sirens screaming. A policeman said that he would need to take a brief statement and Arthur muttered a monotone recollection to the man, who scribbled furiously into a notebook.

Arthur couldn't recall who had telephoned his wife, nor if she had been phoned at all. He did recall telling a policeman where she was that morning and he remembered looking up from the floor, where he had remained crouched since the emergency services had left. The neighbours were in the kitchen, not knowing what should be done and the front door remained wide open. Arthur stood upright, entirely emotionless, as Mary lunged at him. He raised his hands to protect his face from her onslaught, as nails broke through his defences, gouging strips of flesh from his face, as she cursed and swore at her husband.

"How could you be so fucking stupid?" she demanded of him "How, how could you?"

He didn't answer her, nor did he protect himself as her attack slowed and became a half-hearted beating of his chest with clenched fists as, with each thump she sobbed a word. "How... fucking ... stupid ... how ... fucking ... stupid?"

They never spoke to each other again and Arthur never really spoke to anyone again. He talked, but only when it was absolutely necessary. His employers were very sympathetic, telling him that he could take as long as he needed to return to work. Six months later, it became apparent that he would never return and they "let him go".

Mary moved away from the area and took up a post at a school in the Eastern Cape. The house was sold and proceeds split equally. Arthur moved into a small bedsit not far from his old house and lived off the proceeds of the divorce settlement. After a couple of years he accepted a job as barman at the same golf club of which he used to be a member, but after a week or two the limelight grew too bright for him and he opted for a lesser job of washing dishes in the kitchen.

The eighties rolled by, as did the nineties. Arthur was the "you see that poor man over there" in the conversation. He kept himself private, rebuffing offers of any form of assistance or therapy. He drifted from worthless job to worthless unemployment, receiving more-than-generous bar tips and Christmas boxes of brandy and cigarettes.

Arthur hooked up another three hooks' worth of cricket netting and then climbed down off his ladder. He was about to move on to another section of net, but changed his mind. He trudged back to the shed and sat down on his light roller seat. He opened the chest and lifted the lid. He opened another bottle of brandy and pressed the light-duty metal top flat in the palm of his hand with his thumb. He took three large gulps of brandy and placed the bottle down between his feet, twirling it in the dust, to make Olympic ring patterns for no reason at all. Resting his elbows on his knees, he placed his head in his hands, running fingers through his thick, greasy grey hair.

"Fucking nets," he said. "Fucking nets."

ANCHOR MAN

Richard unfurled his Genoa and set his Muira Helena on a broad reach out into the clear waters of False Bay. There was a very gentle southeaster blowing five or six knots through his sails and the sun glowed white hot in the cloudless sky of the Western Cape. A peaked cap and sunglasses were an absolute necessity, as the sun attacked on all fronts, shimmering like a dozen dancing Tinkerbells on the surface of the sea in a blinding strip of light that stretched far out into the Indian Ocean.

He'd cut his motor and the only sounds were those of the small waves surrendering their shape to the bow of his yacht as it slowly cut a path through the gentle swell. Seagulls added their cries to the ocean's orchestra and a spinnaker halyard rhythmically spanked the metal mast in tune to the sway of the hull.

Cars and cyclists heading down to Cape Point soon became specs on the road out of Simonstown. It was a perfect summer day in early January … perfect for sailing, perfect for cycling and perfect for living. The wind may pick up a little later in the day, but the windguru website had this weather pattern settled for a couple of days, which was welcome respite from the endless battering of the prevailing wind, that had pumped for almost two weeks, non-stop.

Richard had only been retired for a year or two. At sixty-three he'd been able to hang up his dentist's hat a little earlier than some of his friends and a little later than a couple of others. Approaching her sixty-eighth birthday, Helen had encouraged her husband to ease into retirement gradually by working one day less a week each year since his late fifties. "You may be my toy boy, Richard," she'd joke, "but you're not as young as you were, you know."

Channel 16 crackled as two inaudible voices came over the radio. It sounded like fishermen chatting about the abundance of yellowtail around the point, thought Richard. They shouldn't be using that channel for idle chitchat. He turned the volume down a touch on his handheld and re-sheathed it in the holster next to the Satnav instruments, then he hardened up a little towards Hangklip on the other side of the bay. A large, protruding portion of the mountainous landscape, it stood sentry duty over False Bay and appeared to be permanently shrouded in mist, irrespective of the weather.

Richard seldom sailed solo, but Helen hadn't been feeling up for a day on the water and her wrist was still bandaged from the fall she had in the garden ten days ago. She was lucky it wasn't a break, but none the less, it was still tender and bruised up to her fingers. She wasn't the most active of crew at the best of times, and it was easy to lose one's balance below deck and a rogue wave or inadvertent gibe at the wrong moment would have her doctor tut-tuting, "I told you so, Helen." Coupled with her battered wrist was the fact that Luke's final-year matric exam results were due out today, so Helen thought she'd accompany him back to school, where they would be posted on a board at noon.

Helen's younger sister and brother-in-law had died in a horrific head-on with a petrol tanker almost sixteen years ago, leaving her two-year-old nephew orphaned. Richard and Helen were named as guardians in the will. Despite the will, there was a lot of paperwork and red tape to cut through, not least of which arising from Helen's age. At nearly fifty she was deemed by the authorities to be too old to adopt. Eventually, however, sense prevailed and they adopted Luke and loved him as their own, a task which they threw themselves into wholeheartedly, having been unsuccessful for years in their attempts to start a family. Although neither Helen nor Richard were religious, he had heard her on one occasion refer to the accident and Luke's subsequent adoption as being "God's will". He preferred to call it "fate".

Husband and wife had hardly spoken a harsh word to each other in over thirty-five years of marriage, but Richard's solo sailing was the one topic that could be guaranteed to raise Helen's hackles – and as they grew older, the issue would burn deeper into her psyche. He would argue that four to five knots of wind, a radio, cell phone and all the flares required of a his yacht's certificate of fitness, made the prospect of impending doom at sea less than being hit by the proverbial bus.

Luke drove Helen's Renault to the school, L-plates indicating his level of inexperience. He's failed his driving test three times in the past two months and both occupants were beginning to tire of the people at the test centre, one of whom failed Luke for rolling the car backwards at the start of the test. Given that the car park of the test centre was situated on one of the most level pieces of land in the area, Helen had subsequently embarked on a verbal altercation with the cashier when booking Luke's next attempt.

He parked the car proficiently enough to have passed the parallel parking had it been another test, then he and Helen made their way to the school's reception area, where a throng of people had already gathered. The five-minute wait for noon was an eternity, but as the secretary opened the doors to the hall, the wait had been worth every second. The provincial Education Department decreed that all results should be made public at noon, so throughout the province, past pupils were straining their necks and scouring the notice boards to see on which rung of the educational ladder they were standing.

Of the one hundred and eighty pupils to sit the matric exams at his school, Luke did not have far to look for his name on the list; starting at the top, he stopped and beamed a telling grin. His name was third from the top, in order of success. With six distinctions from his eight subjects, Luke had secured his place at Stellenbosch University that year to read his chosen subject of law. He would be sure to let Richard know as soon as possible, as promised.

Richard's phone was on and near to hand, but poor reception in False Bay prevented the news being conveyed at that time. Luke would have to try later, or send an SMS.

Richard tacked Helena and eased the main and foresail just a little, so that the early afternoon sun warmed the small of his back. He'd not planned his sail with any specific destination in mind that day, entering 'False Bay' in the log book at the yacht club before he left, which was common practice and merely meant that it would be a returning day trip and not a cruise further up the coast to Mossel Bay, or round the point to Hout Bay or even Cape Town.

It was calm enough to warrant taking a look at Smitswinkel Bay, which lay halfway between Simonstown and Cape Point. It was a very secluded little cove, with a handful of cottages dotted about the place and no access from the winding road above. It was a good half-an-hour hike down to the beach, unless you had a boat … which he had. Yes, Smits it would be. It would require a few more tacks to lay the bay, but he could drop anchor if there wasn't a swell running and maybe have a cup of coffee and some rucks, which Helen had baked the day before and packed in a small Tupperware.

Richard was in two minds with regard to dropping anchor or just motor sailing in and around the tiny bay for a while. His hesitancy regarding the former plan was due to it being fairly heavy going for a single hander to winch the anchor up, whilst simultaneously slowly motoring the boat forward into the wind. The anchor winch was motorised and he'd managed it plenty of times before with Helen on board. She hadn't really contributed much to the task in the past, so Richard decided that he'd basically always anchored solo, anyway. It could become tricky, however, if the wind got up suddenly, so he'd have to keep an eye out for that.

Luke had decided to go off with a few friends for a lunchtime drink, having driven his mother home in the Renault and hopped into another car that also belonged to a parent. Grant had passed his driving test mid-way through the previous year and he was quite happy to follow Luke home and the two of them would meet up with "the crowd" a bit later. Grant was also more than happy to be the designated driver and play taxi later in the day. It would be the ever-popular Peddlars On The Bend for a few beers, and then out again that evening for a bit of a party and a shared taxi to Amy's home, as that would be the cheapest taxi fare back to a bed, sofa, or floor. They'd think about how they all got home from there tomorrow. Luke tried to phone his dad but there was no reply, so once again he sent the same message regarding his results, finishing with a sunglass smiley and an x.

The wind was dropping in False Bay, instruments registering a mere four to five knots, barely enough to fill the sails, but Richard was in no hurry so resisted firing up his engine and shattering the tranquillity of the moment. A couple of dolphins shadowed the vessel, but gave up the game after a few minutes as they preferred to duck and dive around a boat that offered a bit more of a challenge. When the southeaster really puffed and Helena was cranking up eight knots of boat speed, the dolphins would cruise either side, under and about the craft, almost mocking the crew and their inability to perform with the balletic grace and ease of their aquatic companions.

Smitswinkel Bay was calm, clear and at its beautiful best. Richard had never known it to be so still. He was about three hundred metres off shore and by now he would usually hear the waves breaking on the bright white, sand beach. Breaking waves were no more than a swish, as sand, pebbles and shells merely rocked to and fro in the ripples that gently kissed the shore. The fynbos backdrop on the granite escarpment towered above the rustic cottages and the matchstick holidaymakers playing ball in the shallows.

Richard reluctantly started the motor and chugged slowly forward into the bay. The motor was a noisy necessity, as the boat was gently entering the lee of the land and the little wind that he'd enjoyed up until then was now no more than a light breeze. The conditions were perfect to drop anchor and soak up the day … perhaps read a chapter or two; have a dip in the cool blue waters. To motor back and forth around the bay would be to destroy the very essence of Smits, where people came to cut loose the shackles of work and rein in the hectic pace of modern-day living.

Luke, Grant and several other ex-pupil friends from various Western Cape schools were celebrating their results. Grant was beginning to tire of the taste and sweetness of carbonated drinks, whilst the others showed no such symptoms, as one beer led to three and beer was substituted with rum and black. By late afternoon, peppermint shots were doing the rounds and Amy was kneeling over the porcelain in a ladies' cubicle. Grant decided that one beer would "do no harm" and accepted another when told that "You can get away with two, if you are stopped."

Helena eased into the lee of a rocky outcrop protruding from the southerly end of the bay, allowing enough distance between boat and rock should a one-eighty swing occur later. Richard furled the Genoa and luffed the main, before heading to the bow and lifting the heavy anchor from the chain locker and sliding it under the pulpit. Careful not to catch his fingers in the several metres of chain, the following anchor rope was released in a controlled, but swift manner, descending to its resting place in seconds. It was fairly shallow at about eight metres below the keel and the yacht drifted back slowly, until the rope jerked taught, indicating that the anchor had bitten. A touch astern on the engine drove the anchor deeper into its sandy host. Richard restored calm to the bay as he cut the engine, dropped the main and wrapped it in a couple of sail ties for neatness. A pair of hopeful seagulls dropped in to see if there were any titbits on offer and squawked their appreciation when a handful of rusks was tossed their way.

Coffee, rusks and the latest edition of a sailing magazine kept Richard occupied for the best part of the afternoon, though he contemplated a swim on a couple of occasions, as the heat of the sun seemed to funnel into the shimmering bay.

Helen's afternoon had comprised attending to the needs of her herb garden and then dozing off in a deck chair under the shade of her vine-covered pergola. Her newspaper lay by her side and she awoke around five o'clock as a sudden gust of wind collected up her Cape Times and danced it around her patio. It had suddenly got chilly and the freshening wind had a bite to it. She went inside and put the pages of her paper back together, before calling Luke and then Richard. There was no reply from either phone and she felt a shiver run through her body.

Grant's car contained more than he'd cared to drive – one front passenger named Luke was fine, but four rowdy friends, including two giggly girls, was definitely four rowdy friends too many. He was finding it difficult to think and twice yelled at them via his rear-view mirror as they headed home. The green light allowed him to proceed at the intersection and the red should have halted the oncoming truck, which was travelling across his path at almost twice the permitted speed. The truck driver knew that to brake hard now could cause his load to jackknife, so as the light turned orange, he slammed his foot hard down on the accelerator, in the hope of reducing the amount of "red time" he had left.

"Guys, please!" shouted Grant, as the green light signalled its intent and he shifted into first. "Hey, I've asked you nicely, for fucksake!"

Richard decided to pack up for the day and prepared to up anchor and head for home. He hoisted the main, which flapped vigorously in the freshening breeze. He turned the engine over and, mentally rehearsed the procedure ahead. The wind would blow him away from the rocks, but he'd have to steer towards the anchor in order to loosen and raise it.

He wished he'd departed fifteen minutes earlier, as the wind was picking up by the minute. Next to the tiller was a small black lever, which he gently pushed to port. It should have allowed Helena to edge upwind and allow him to reel in the anchor rope and chain.

Instead, there was an almighty shudder, which had Richard instinctively returning the lever to neutral, whilst cursing his bad luck with several mumbled expletives. A thousand possibilities raced through his mind at once, none of which was of any comfort to the old man. The answer was simple, as would be the solution, hopefully. He cursed again as he shaded his eyes from the setting sun and leaned astern to look deep down into the waters and to his propeller. It was still there, or at least he presumed it was … wrapped up in a shroud of dark brown kelp.

He should have checked for that, and he berated himself for the failing. "Stupid … bloody stupid," he said, but it was too late for recriminations. He had to fix it and soon.

A long tube of kelp with dark green fronds had sneaked up on him while he was at anchor. There was a fair amount of it about and he'd always been careful to avoid it. There was a large portion surrounding the rock and quite a bit standing sentry on the opposite side of the bay, but this must have been a partially submerged section, that had worked its way loose. He had a mask and snorkel, but had left his fins back at the house. His pulse began to race, as he switched off the engine and went below to find his snorkelling gear. He'd always kept some diving kit on board for such situations, but had only ever used it for recreational purposes.

"Look out!" screamed Luke as Grant slammed on the brakes, bringing one of the girls forward into his headrest with such a thump that he felt it reverberate throughout his seat. A large beer truck came thundering past them, roaring one long and deafening blast of the horn. The occupants of the Renault sat motionless, as following cars tooted at them, seemingly oblivious to their close encounter with fate. The rest of their journey home was in comparative silence. One girl had a bloody nose, but she wasn't the one crying. The guys in the back sobered in an instant and one of them just repeated what everyone knew already. They were very lucky to be alive and the driver of the truck was a moron. Luke just said "Jesus" several times and shook his head.

The sweat on Richard's forehead trickled down his temples and dripped from his nose, as he climbed up the steps and exited the yacht. He stood aft and held onto the back stays, whist surveying the scene below. He had a serrated dive knife, which would make light work of the kelp, but the sea was getting choppy and conditions were making his task all the more worrying.

He lowered the stainless-steel ladder that rested on the transom next to the rudder, then took a deep breath and plunged feet first overboard. The water was colder than he'd anticipated and it nearly sucked the air clean from his lungs. As he surfaced for air, he instinctively sucked on his snorkel before blowing it dry. He coughed and spluttered as the salty water raced down his throat. He stretched out for the ladder, but missed, as the bottom rung lifted beyond his reach. Another lunge had him grappling with the second rung of the seven available, but that was prized from his grip as the boat lurched skywards on another wave. Richard was panicking and he could knew that the situation required a cool head.

He swam a short distance away from the boat, scissor-kicking frantically to tread water as best he could without the aid of fins. He bobbed up and down, riding a few waves and breathing steadily through his snorkel before heading back to Helena. He managed to grasp the back of the rudder and ride the ups and downs with his boat, before taking three large breaths and lowering himself down the rudder.

The mask was not a tight fit and water began to seep in, forcing Richard to snort and blow precious air through his nose to clear his vision. He hacked at a piece of kelp twice, but was forced to surface for air as his lungs cried out for relief. In his youth, he'd been able to free dive for what seemed like ages, but now he was only able to stay down for seconds. His buoyancy was not playing ball and he found himself using up all his energy just trying to keep upright. One particularly heavy swell turned him upside down and had him frantically thrashing for the surface, oblivious to which direction it was.

Battling for breath, but more for the strength to complete his task, Richard was beginning to feel exhausted. Three, four, five times he repeatedly inched his way down to the propeller, wedging a hand in between rudder and hull for stability. His arms and legs were scratched and bleeding and his fingers were growing numb with cold.

A large piece of kelp was loosened and ripped away by the surge, only to reveal another piece strangling the prop shaft. He summoned all his reserves and dived straight down to tackle the serpent below, hacking away furiously at the rubbery foe. His hand was cramping, but he had enough left in his lungs for one final assault of the partially severed piece of kelp. But as he changed hands, the numb fingers of his left hand let him down and the knife plummeted to the sea floor. The boat lurched and suddenly lifted Richard several feet, almost ripping the snorkel from his mouth. He needed air and blindly kicked for the surface, with arms by his side and not stretched skyward.

The stainless-steel ladder, lowered earlier as a potential saviour, had not been secured properly by its owner, who had forgotten to insert the steel pin, that kept it fastened. Hinged at the top only, the ladder was free to follow whichever direction nature dictated. As the yacht tossed and pitched in the swell it swung out from the stern, only to crash back into the boat seconds later. Richard surfaced and gasped for air, as the bottom rung of the ladder swung out and crashed down from a giddy height onto the bridge of his nose; splitting his mask and sending him back under with the full force of the boat in free fall.

Richard thrashed and kicked through the salty red mist that was before his eyes. His nose was broken and a deep gash across his face was spewing inky red clouds of blood into the churning sea.

He surfaced again and tried to float on his back, but was swamped by wave after wave, as the sea turned on him and he slowly slipped beyond consciousness.

Earlier that afternoon, an elderly woman with binoculars had been watching the yacht in the bay, as well as the people on the beach. That was her entertainment, as it has been for almost twenty years. Later in the day, she'd returned to her lounge overlooking the sea, just in time to notice the white horses prancing on the water, further out to sea. The wind was getting up and that yacht was heading back to Simonstown, no doubt. She'd watched as the sailor had struggled with something or other on the boat and then minutes later decided to go for a swim. By the time she'd decided that he was in trouble and had notified her neighbour, the events had unfolded and Richard was gasping for his last breaths.

Sea Rescue station No. 10 was alerted and dispatched, but it took nearly an hour for them to scramble and reach Smitswinkel. Helena was attached to a line, her anchor retrieved and she was taken back to the marina, where Luke and Helen anxiously awaited news.

The search-and-rescue operation would become a recovery operation the following day. Richard's body was washed ashore not far from his anchorage and paramedics wearily stretchered his body up the footpath leading to the road.

Helen never set sail again and seldom spoke of the day the sea took her husband away. Luke studied law and chose to block out all memories of the day his exam results were published.

Several days after the accident, Richard's belongings were returned to the family. Helen put his wristwatch and car keys to one side, along with his cell phone. Instinctively, she picked up the phone and went to his messages. There were three from her that afternoon, together with one from Luke. She wiped her eyes with the back of her hand and scrolled down the message.

Hi Dad, got the grades I needed. Can never thank you and Mum enough 4 everything. Luv u lotz and c u soon. x.

Oh, and there was a smiley face with sunglasses.

Richard was always a straight smiley and Luke's smiley always wore shades.

ANYONE FOR SQUASH?

A short run around his usual route after work, followed by a couple of drinks with his friends at the golf club, would round off the week quite nicely for James Mitchell. It had been a very full week on the work front at Taylor Meredith & Partners, accountants to multinational corporates and an ideal company for James to achieve his goals and climb the last few rungs of the ladder to full partner. At twenty-eight he was an Associate with aspirations to obtain what no one had before him – Partner before thirty.

James was the product of the best private school education Cape Town could offer; only Bishops was good enough for the son of John and Judith Mitchell from Southern Cross Drive, Constantia. The Mitchells had all gone to Bishops.

James left his beamer in one of the few vacant underground parking bays at the gym and headed for the changing rooms. A five-kilometre run and a couple of circuits of weights would do nicely. Though not a vain man by gym standards, he allowed himself to pause briefly before one of the full-length mirrors dotted about between the lockers. At just over six foot, well toned and enough of a tan to compliment his surfer-blond hair, James' looks caused many a head to turn at the gym, in the office and most other places he frequented. If it weren't for Taylor Meredith, he'd have worn his hair shoulder length and indulged in a body piercing or two, just to cause a tut and a gasp in Upper Constantia circles.

His run took him from the gym, across a busy dual carriageway and then out over a field into pine woods, where undulating cycle tracks reminded him of those school cross-country runs they endured for sport and punishment. How he'd hated being forced into cross country; forced to do anything. Now, ten years later he enjoyed his exercise, he enjoyed his sport. He played golf every Saturday and tennis most Sunday mornings, weather permitting. Some of his married friends battled to get out at the weekend for a round of golf, let alone golf and tennis. "Marriage," muttered James, as he sprinted through a gap in the fence and off across the field, "Not for me." His six-month relationship with Heather was very much a casual thing – well, he thought of it that way. She was there when it suited and she knew not to interfere with his plans to … well, to do whatever James Mitchell wanted to do. Life was good.

James felt light on his feet and upped the pace above the usual. His niggling leg injury seemed fine. He would push himself, build up a good sweat and then the golf club beers would slip down even better. As he ran, head down, looking out for the rogue tree root or branch that could be his undoing, he felt a twinge in his right hamstring. The same bloody hamstring he'd pulled a couple of weeks ago, reaching for a cross-court return of serve from his tennis buddy, Derrick. He uttered an expletive, but carried on, having eased back his pace a little. It was just a twinge, but he could feel it pulling, as he ran with shorter strides. As he jogged, James became aware of a misty haze, which was not so much descending, as appearing, forming around him in a swirling dance that shortened his stride and slowed his pace even more. He stopped his run abruptly for fear of encountering a tree or running headlong into thick bush, as the mist turned to thick, blinding white fog, the like of which, he'd never seen before – not even that November in England a couple of years back. James felt his hamstring, which was tight and uncomfortable. He placed his hand before his eyes, not so much to test the visibility through the white fog, but more to shield his eyes from the intensity of the inexplicable brightness that was growing brighter as the suffocating blanket swirled faster about him, squeezing him in a vortex of whiteness. James battled to hold his footing as the forces against him attempted to displace and lift him from the path underfoot. He tried to drop to his knees, in an attempt to lower his centre of gravity, but it was too late.

Fear gripped him, as his mind raced faster than the phenomenon twisting and twirling around him … spinning him and lifting him. As his feet slowly parted company from the earth beneath, the vortex took charge and spun his body round, as if he were a plastic shopping bag caught in a tornado. He made a desperate lunge to free himself from the grip of the force, but only succeeded in falling forward, face first, arms pinned to his side, as if bound by a whale-bone straitjacket. James waited for his face to come crashing down to the pine forest floor, bloodied face and broken nose. But nothing happened. Instead, he just kept falling, but this time head over heels, faster and faster, his mind torn apart with fear and anticipation of the unknown fate ahead of him.

Thoughts of death, bright lights at the end of a tunnel and unfinished business, all mingled with the rigid fear of the unknown and ignorance of what he was going through. He was dying and there was nobody to help him, no last words, no mother or father at his bedside and no doctors to tell him what he was dying of. He drifted into a coma. No thoughts, no dreams … just a bright white nothingness, which seemed to last an eternity.

James lay on his back. He could feel the cold ground of the cycle track under his vest. He opened his eyes to see a thick carpet of evergreen pine tops, beyond which puffy white clouds raced across blue skies.

"What the bloody … what was …" he said out loud, unable to finish his words, or comprehend what had just transpired. He sat up and felt the back of his head for bumps, bruises or blood, but found nothing. He surveyed his knees bent up before his eyes, but they were fine, no cuts. He pressed two fingers deep into the back of his right leg, expecting to flinch from the pain of his strained hamstring, but there was no such pain. He felt as good as he had done five minutes or five days before, better than he had if you take into account the leg. Bloody odd, he thought ... odd and worrying. Maybe he'd had a stroke, but it didn't feel like he thought that should feel.

"Hey! ... hey! ... hey!" he shouted, just to see if he could. He felt completely, utterly ... normal.

James jogged the two or three kilometres back to the gym, but opted for fifteen minutes in the steam room, rather than the pre-planned circuits, for no reason other than maybe his "turn for the worse" had been exercise induced. He'd take it easy for an hour or two.

The sun was setting as James drove up the ramp and out of the gym complex. From the corner of his eye, he sensed something different as he took a left at the traffic lights and doubled back past the gym and adjoining squash courts. He didn't have time for a double take, as the traffic was busy and the taxi in front of him warranted his full attention.

The golf club was only a five-minute drive from the gym and his home was the same distance back again, past the gym. No danger of roadblocks or breathalysers on that stretch of road, but he usually restricted himself to his own limit of three beers at the golf club.

Derrick was sitting on a stool in his usual little corner of the bar, much as he was every Friday evening about that time. Standing next to him were Peter, Dave and Chris, all with beer in hand, chatting as usual about who was in which four ball the following day, or the full cleavage on display across the room.

"Hi, guys," said James, easing his way into the gap in the circle that appeared on his arrival. "Can I get anyone anything?"

"You could get me a kilo of those, Jimbo," said Derrick, indicating with raised eyebrows and a nod of his head towards the full-breasted woman, who was aware of the attention her unbuttoned blouse was attracting.

"I'll take that as a no, then," said James, thanking the barman, who had already set an Amstel down on the bar top.

"Cheers, chaps," James continued, clinking his friends' bottles and draining half the contents of his Amstel in three large gulps.

"Teeing off at twelve-ten tomorrow, James," said Derrick. "It's me and you, and we are going to take Pete and Dave to the cleaners. Don't be late."

"Am I ever?" James retorted, "And are you OK for tennis on Sunday morning?"

"Who's she?" replied Derrick.

"Funny! Who's she, what?" said James. "Seriously, Derrick. Ten o'clock Sunday morning. Are we still on?" Derrick looked a little puzzled, as did the rest of the group.

"So? What's the punch line, James?" asked Chris. "Is it one of those 'knock, knock, who's there? Tellis. Tellis who?' jokes of yours?"

James just shook his head. "Maybe I'll come back in and start again, by which time you'll have had your fun. Anyway, where were we?"

The subject matter of the conversation swung round to cricket for the majority, while Dave and Chris chatted about some committee issue, which was of little interest to James. He had one or two more than his usual three beers and put thoughts of his earlier run behind him. He was going to mention it to the boys, but not in their present mood, or after he'd had five beers. Besides, he didn't know how to explain the event to himself, let alone anyone else.

"Right, I'm off," James announced. "I'll see you guys on the tee tomorrow and maybe I can get a sensible answer from you about the tennis, Derrick." All James got out of his friend was some comment about not being able to take his drink like he used to ... a chuckle from the others and that was it. James left the bar a little irritated by the whole conversation, but content in the knowledge that he'd get a straight answer tomorrow on the first tee.

It was pitch dark as James drove back past the gym and he had drunk five, or was it six beers, so he couldn't possibly have seen what looked like an extension to the squash courts building. He slowed his car and peered into the night about fifty metres off the road. It looked as if, where once there had been a building containing four tennis courts, there was now a building at least twice as long and wide, where four of the six courts had been. It must be an illusion and there was some idiot driving up his arse, so he'd not bother turning around to check it out.

James was restless that night, waking several times, which was most unusual for him. The little sleep he did get was filled with dreams about the woods, the mist and falling into white space. By the time the sun came up, he was in a deep sleep, falling once more into nothingness. He was about to hit the ground, but was prevented by the timely intervention of his alarm clock. His T-shirt and shorts were soaking wet and he wiped the sweat from his brow with bed linen, leaving a visible damp patch on the light blue cotton sheet. His newspaper was retrieved from his front step, as coffee percolated and hissed in the kitchen, filling his apartment with the aroma of Italian Superior Blend. James took coffee, toast and the Cape Times back to bed. He glanced at the headlines, and then worked his way back through the sport on the back pages. Tiger was bouncing back into form. Messi was about to sign a new deal at Barcelona. Wimbledon was just around the corner, so James looked to see who was in the finals of the various grass court tournaments that abounded throughout Europe around this time of the year. He searched not once, but over and over. Nothing. Not even in the results section. There was, however a large photo of some badminton player and a quarter-page write-up next to it headlining Badminton World Cup triumph! "Whatever next? Bloody useless paper," he muttered to himself, discarding it on the carpet next to his bed. He got dressed and decided a more substantial breakfast was in order, making enough bacon, eggs and baked beans for two. Sky News sports was just as useless with regard to their coverage of tennis, so he watched the tail end of Ground Hog Day. It was his all-time favourite movie and he never tired of telling his friends that he could "watch that movie over and over and over again". They had long since grown fed up with that one.

An hour and a bit to tee-off time. James thought he'd surprise his playing partner and get down there a little early, rather than his usual sprint to the first tee. He'd hit a few drives on the range and maybe spend twenty minutes on the practice putting green.

As James drove back past the gym, he suddenly remembered the night before. He scarcely believed his eyes, but this time he had to, as it was a beautiful sunny day and he was stone cold sober. The squash courts were big enough to cater for at least ten courts and from what he could see from the road, the tennis courts had been turned into either additional parking, or swallowed up by the new squash court development.

"How the fuck did that happen?" he asked himself out loud, making an ungainly U-turn, before heading back into the road leading to the gym. He had to take a closer look, even if it meant sacrificing his session on the practice green. He drove into the car park and slowed to almost walking pace as he pulled up and parked his car in a bay, which not two days before had been one of the two grass courts. The four clay courts were also gone. He blinked not once, but several times, thinking this may somehow restore normality to a seriously confusing situation. He gingerly got out of his car, forgetting to close the door behind. An elderly caretaker stood a few metres away, brushing leaves into a small pile at the far corner of the car park, where it abutted the almost palatial squash courts.

"Excuse me!" shouted James. "Excuse … um … hey" he repeated, making his way towards the man. He spun his whole body around whilst walking, as if looking for a lost helium balloon. He was unsure as to exactly how to phrase the question.

The man halted his sweeping and dropped his boom to the ground. "Yes, sir? What's the problem?"

"Um … nothing, but um … how long has this been here? I mean it wasn't … this," said James, pointing to the squash courts.

"Don't know exactly," replied the bemused worker. "As long as I can remember. Got a bit of a facelift a couple of years back, I guess … " but James wasn't hearing anything the man had to say.

"No ... no … he persisted. "I mean when, no … where are the tennis courts?" he blurted out.

"The what courts?"

"Tennis. Tennis courts!"

"Sorry, sir, I really must get on," said the visibly confused old man. He turned his back before bending down to pick up his broom; then hurriedly headed off muttering something inaudible under his breath, abandoning the pile of leaves he had so carefully gathered.

James just stood there for a full two minutes, gazing at the squash courts, then tarmac car park and back to the courts. The building was even bigger and more opulent than it looked from the road. Much, much bigger. He ambled across to the building's entrance. It was a truly magnificent structure, with a spacious double-volume reception, where one of two pretty receptionists greeted him as he entered through the automatic revolving doors.

"Can I help you, sir?" asked the brunette. She was just James' type and on any other day, he may have been inclined to flirt with her, but not today. His face was ashen and his mouth hung open, giving the appearance of one who was not quite in control of his faculties. The walls of the reception were lined at the back with what looked like teak panelling of the highest-quality craftsmanship. He was treading on white Carrara marble flooring and high above him a spectacular arrangement of low-voltage down lights mimicked celestial bodies in a beautiful dome ceiling. The walls were lined with photos, memorabilia and trophies from what were obviously major squash tournaments held somewhere; but where? One such photo hung to the left of the granite-topped reception desk. It caught James' eye, as it was a magnificent aerial photo of what appeared to be the Cape Town Stadium, but in the middle of the playing surface was a single glass squash court. The stadium was floodlit and filled to capacity, with several huge TV screens strategically placed around the arena. The photo appeared to have been snapped in the middle of a match, as the big screens were showing a close-up of a player at full stretch.

"Thanks, no ... or rather, yes please. Can I take a look around?" he replied nervously, as would an adolescent schoolboy to a young female teacher for whom he had a burning desire. He felt the blood in his face flush hot and fast, as the girl pointed to a set of double doors and told him that wouldn't be a problem. James entered through the doors, expecting to see the usual squash courts with flaking paint, worn timber board-flooring and tired, threadbare carpet tiles. Instead, he looked down on an arena below him the like of which he's never seen before. The single court with glass walls was no different to that found in any self-respecting sports club, but this one was obviously sunk below the natural ground level to accommodate the terraced seating all around. Enough for maybe five thousand spectators ... for squash? James was on the middle tier; a main walkway from which rose many levels of cushioned seats above him and down to the court below him. It was truly amazing. TV cameras were permanently fixed in position all around the arena, as were large screens and speakers. He was about to venture beyond, to see what lay through the doors on the far side, as quite clearly, from what he saw outside, there were more facilities to be seen.

"Shit," he said. "Bloody hell, golf." He was late again. He raced out of the building, thanking the receptionist as he went, his mind spinning in a confused state. Was he dreaming, or maybe in a coma? Perhaps he was mentally ill and people were keeping it from him. The anxieties of the white-light run from the day before returned to him, as his heart pumped blood through his bulging veins and he felt slightly giddy. He left rubber in the car park, as he sped off for the first tee. He'd have to forego the driving range and the putting green, but should make it just in time.

James arrived panting and sweating as he ran the last few metres down the brick pathway, catching a wheel of his cart in the flower bed, tipping irons out of his bag in the process. The other three had teed off and James promptly hooked his drive out of bounds.

"Relax, old boy. Relax," said Derrick, less concerned with his partner's well-being than the prospect of losing the sizeable bet he had placed on behalf of himself and partner, not thirty minutes earlier. James played three off the tee and watched his ball roll into a sand trap on the adjoining fairway.

"Bollocks," he said out loud.

The golf didn't improve for James and whilst Derrick did his best to hold the fort, Pete and Dave enjoyed the handshake on the eighteenth green much more than their opposition. James had probably played one of his worst rounds of golf for some years, preoccupied with thoughts of squash, tennis, running, falling, everything except golf. Nothing was making sense.

"How's the hammy then, Jimbo?" asked Derrick, placing three Amstels and a Heineken on the table. The "hammy" was fine; he couldn't feel a thing and just gestured with a thumbs-up sign.

"So, you can't blame that then!" Derrick said. "You are bloody quiet today ... what's up?"

He was right, James couldn't blame that, but neither could he blame it on the fact that he thought he was going crazy, due to the fact that a multi-million mega-bucks squash facility had been built on the site of the local tennis courts – and in only two days! It was time to test the water again.

"I'm fine, Derrick, really. In fact I'm fine enough to whip your arse in two sets tomorrow, if we can find a court."

"Two sets of what? Badgers?" laughed Derrick who, along with the other two, thought that to be a pretty funny retort. Derrick laughed out loud whilst James remained poker faced.

"Tennis ... tennis ... tennis ... fucking tennis!" yelled James, slamming his beer down on the table, as a blanket of silence fell over the crowded bar.

"Steady on, mate," said Derrick, a look of concern replacing the laughter lines. James' beer frothed and overflowed onto the table top, but not enough to threaten the carpet. "I don't know what I said, but I didn't get your joke, that's all. Sorry, James."

James regained his composure, but tears welled up and blurred his vision. It was all he could do to get the words "excuse me" out, before two tears rolled down his cheeks. The bar was still, as no one moved, or uttered a sound. James stood and calmly walked out of the door. Pete rose and tried to catch him by the arm, but Dave caught Peter with a little tug of his sweater and James was gone.

The drive to Western Province Club usually took about fifteen minutes. He was a member there. It too had squash, tennis, hockey, cricket … you name it. James got there in about ten minutes. There was still an hour and a bit of light left. His stomach churned as he entered the sports complex. The club house was as he knew it. Built about ten years ago, it was exactly as it should be. But the tennis courts were no longer there; gone … replaced by a similar-size building to the one he'd visited at the gym earlier that day. A sprawling complex totally glazed in reflective "Solarshield" glass, probably twice the size of the club house, with a large back-lit signage panel proclaiming Western Province Squash Academy.

He scanned his membership card and walked into the clubhouse, up to the club sports shop, which was closed, but surrounded by glass shop frontage on three sides, giving an unobstructed view of the equipment on view. Hockey sticks, cricket bats, pads, basket balls. A few badminton rackets were hung from the display opposite him and beside them row upon row of squash rackets. "Squash, squash, squash," said James, not a single tennis racket in sight. "Nothing, but bloody squash."

James returned to his car and dialled a number.

"Heather?" he said. "I need to talk to you. Yes, it is quite important. No, I'm fine. No, it's not about us, or you … I just need to talk to you about something. Eight, yes. My place."

James drove home slowly. He'd nearly collided with a taxi on the way through to Western Province Club, by dicing at a set of lights.

He closed his front door and opened the fridge, throwing the bottle top towards the waste paper bin, but missing. He sat at his desk and opened his laptop. Launch browser … Google … type.

[Tennis]

[Do you mean Trellis?]

"No, I don't mean bloody trellis" he said, tapping away at the keyboard.

[Wimbledon] – search.

[Suburb of London]

"That's it! Suburb of London!" Tap, tap, tap. "I don't believe this."

[Raphael Nadal] "Ah, something. Wikipedia … yes, with photos. That's him," exclaimed James, visibly elated.

[Raphael "Rafa" Nadal – Spanish. born : 3rd June 1986 is a professional soccer player for Real Madrid…]. James had no more to give … he was emotionally drained. Roger Federer was punched into Google, but gave nothing back, as was the case with Jimmy Connors, McEnroe, Laver and Steffi Graf.

James turned off his laptop and stared into space. He downed his beer and then another. The doorbell rang. It was Heather and he hadn't even prepared himself for her visit. Would she laugh at him? Would she think as the others had, that this was just another one of his silly jokes?

Heather looked stunning. The receptionist at the squash club, thought James. He knew that she'd reminded him of someone. It was Heather, but he'd been so engrossed, he'd not clicked. Heather put her arms around him and gave him a lingering, slow kiss. At least that hadn't changed. God, she was a sexy little thing, he thought … slender and beautifully proportioned. Light as a feather, with dark brown eyes and brown hair worn pageboy style.

He led her by the hand to the kitchen, where he popped two beers. She followed him into the lounge, where they sat side by side on the couch.

"Cheers!" he said. Heather echoed the word, but she felt uneasy. Was this going to be the "let's just stay friends" sermon she'd been dreading?

James had been thinking furiously about his opening line. He braced himself and took a deep breath.

"Heather. Now don't laugh, promise?"

"Promise."

"Well," he continued, "I've invented what I think could be a pretty shit-hot game. You know how that guy a few years back invented the windsurfer and then we had those sea kites, or whatever they are called?"

"Kiteboarding," she said.

"Yes, that," he said, shuffling his bum on the sofa. "Well, my idea isn't about a new water sport. It's a bit like a cross between squash and badminton. I don't know, let's call it … um tennis, for want of a better word." James stared hard into Heather's eyes for the fainted flicker of recognition at the "T" word. There was none.

"OK." she said softly. "Tennis it is."

"Right," James continued, clearing his throat with a nervous little cough. "It's played on grass; on a court a bit bigger than badminton and with balls instead of shuttlecocks. The balls are soft and bouncy and covered with fur."

"Kinky! A bit like yours then," said Heather who, upon seeing the expression on James' face, followed up with a quick "Sorry."

"One player serves, as in squash, but overhead and into a square on the other side of the net. The ball can only bounce once on each side. If you get it past your opponent, the score is fifteen love … or nil … love… nil," said James, wishing he'd kept the scoring system a little simpler. He was getting frustrated, as her expression glazed over. It was useless. How on earth could he explain this to anyone who didn't have a clue what he was talking about? It even sounded ridiculous to him, as he was trying to explain it. The scoring … Jesus, the scoring and the fact that you need ball boys stationed around the court, just to throw four or five balls to a player, who then selects two, throws the others away, and uses only one.

"Never mind," said James. "I give up." It was useless.

James and Heather went to bed and after making love, James lay awake, wide awake, turning over in his mind the events of the last twenty-four hours. It had seemed like an eternity. He tried to make sense of it all. Was he going insane, like in that Discovery programme he watched about Alzheimer's, or whatever it was? Or was that swirling bright light in the woods a portal, linking two parallel universes? That had been the subject of a recent Stephen Hawking documentary that had so fascinated him a few weeks ago. Mad or portal? Portal … mad? Maybe tennis was a figment of his imagination, conjured up by a disturbed comatose mind. Either way, there was nothing he could do about it and no one to turn to.

Two sleepless nights finally caught up with James and he drifted off at about five in the morning. Heather made breakfast and brought it to the bedroom, where the aroma of scrambled eggs, bacon and coffee woke him from more of the same inexplicable dreams.

"Are you playing badminton with Derrick today?" she asked.

James just groaned and rolled over onto the paper that had accompanied his breakfast. He skirted through the back pages, but wasn't surprised to see that the Stormers had won the day before, India had beaten Sri Lanka in a one-dayer, Noel Jenkins was the number 1-ranked squash player in the world and Malaysia had easily won the Badminton World Cup in Kuala Lumpur.

James picked up the phone from the side table and dialled a number as Heather placed the tray to one side and wedged herself in on the edge of the mattress.

"Hello, Derrick. Listen, sorry about yesterday at the club … just a bit of pent-up stress from the office … wrong time of the month, maybe. Anyway … sorry. Um … I was wondering, are you up for a game of … of … badminton, or squash in about an hour?"

DICKO AND THE DOG

One Sunday lunchtime in mid-autumn, Dicko found himself somewhat bored with the way his day was panning out. Having recently moved in with his girlfriend Jackie, he was happy enough with their little cottage in the village of Monkton Combe, just outside Bath. Dicko's fondness of dogs was on a par with that of his local postman, so it was with more than a little surprise that Jackie had agreed to his suggestion that he take her beloved corgi for her daily walk. Lizzie was a feisty little bitch with a propensity to yelp at the slightest provocation, not unlike her owner in that regard.

Julian Dixon, affectionately known as "Dicko" to his friends, was six foot four inches tall, had the makings of a well-earned beer belly and was the proud owner of an extravagantly long, curly black beard. If anybody was looking for a character to play the part of Moses in a Hollywood epic, then (beer belly aside) Dicko would have been a serious candidate. An Oxford underachiever of some note (well, third-year Oxford drop-out to be more precise, as he'd never even given himself a chance to achieve), Dicko had seldom taken anything in his life seriously. So, had he been cast in the role of Moses, the odds would have been heavily stacked in favour of him sleeping in on the first day of filming.

Dicko dressed himself accordingly for a long walk in the English countryside, leashing the anxious Lizzie and wrapping himself in a thick grey overcoat and eight-foot-long green-and-white Plymouth Argyle scarf, which circumnavigated his neck four times and still trailed over his shoulders and down his back.

He confidently said his goodbyes and set off down the village high street. Not sixty yards from his front door, Dicko took a sharp right turn, wiped his wellies on the coir doormat and entered the double-leaf doors of the Wheelwright Arms, stooping to avoid an encounter with the nineteenth-century doorframe. It was noon and this popular little pub was just beginning to fill up with its usual Sunday lunchtime patrons. Dicko had been a border at the nearby elite boys' school, lived in and around the area over the years and was a well-known character to most of the traditional beer-quaffing community. Within minutes, he was sitting on a barstool downing his second pint, entertaining acquaintances with his quick wit and Richie Benaud impersonations. Lizzie was resigned to her fate, tethered to the leg of a nearby table, grovelling for the odd pork scratching or crisp.

A young barmaid, keen to impress the landlord on her first day of work, marched over to Dicko's ensemble, which was getting louder by the pint.

"Ooze dog is this 'un?" she said, trying to make herself heard above the crowd. Nobody was listening.

"Ere. No dogs allowed in 'ere. Them's the rules. 'Oo owns this dog?" she repeated.

"It's mine," Dicko said, looking straight past the unfortunate girl. "What's the problem, Miss?"

"No dogs, I said. Them's the rules," she said, increasingly aware of the interest being fostered by the debate.

Dicko crossed his eyes, looked to the right, looked left and then skyward, avoiding eye contact with the barmaid at all times.

"But, she's my guide dog," he said, eventually.

"Yeah, like 'ell," said the barmaid. "Since when 'as a bloody corgi been a bleedin' guide dog?"
Their little corner of the pub was hushed.

"A corgi?" proclaimed Dicko, at the top of his voice. "A corgi? The bastards have done me again!"

The barmaid was not impressed by the comment and even less so by the teary-eyed landlord ordering her to pour Dicko "a pint of the best on the house".

Several more beers and couple of gins later, the landlord was calling, "Time, gentlemen, please!"
Dicko reached over the bar and helped himself to a small jar of Colman's Hot English Mustard and a teaspoon.

Beckoning Lizzie with a morsel of rejected pork pie that was close by, Dicko seized the dog with one hand and forced a large dollop of mustard into the poor creature's mouth. With that, he calmly took charge of the whingeing corgi and smartly strode out of the pub, banging the top of his head on the doorframe in the process.

Lizzie was returned panting and salivating to her owner, whereupon Dicko retired to a couch in the lounge and promptly fell asleep in front of the television.

"My, but you are a thirsty girl, Lizzie," said Jackie. "Did you have a nice long walk, then?"

ROLL OF THE DICE

A three-day lull in the prevailing southeaster, had left the sea off the small Western Cape village of Kommetjie, flat, clear and inviting. Ribbons of kelp surfed gentle ripples, pretending to be waves. Tubes of slippery dark green played sea serpent, as they arched above troughs and then dived into the depths of the of chilly blue Atlantic ocean.

Long renowned as a haven for recreational divers, Kommetjie also offered residents and visitors long sandy walks, rock-pool adventures and the chance to let time off the leash and run free to other destinations, where it mattered.

Robin Reynolds was almost a resident, living alone with his single-parent mother in a timber-framed home just on the outskirts of Kommetjie, in the village of Capri, a mere five-minute cycle ride from the sea's edge. Robin and his friend Dillon were in their matric year of school and both were destined for university life the following year.

Mother and son enjoyed the solitude offered by their home. Being set on the hillside overlooking the sea, it was close to the essential amenities, but far enough from civilisation to be considered rural. Their house had been built by the owner of the plot and was once part of small dairy farm. Robin's mother had been renting for three years – three years since her husband had passed away and their circumstances had taken such a dramatic turn.

Shirley Reynolds taught English and Geography at her son's former junior school and the salary allowed them just enough to get by each month, but without any of the luxuries most of her friends took for granted. She was blonde and blue-eyed, but her hair hadn't seen the inside of a salon for an eternity and her eyes no longer sparkled with laughter, the way her son remembered.

Shirley and Robin enjoyed a mutual friendship and bond seldom found between mother and teenager, despite the thirty-five-year age gap. She had long given up hopes of raising a family, so Robin's arrival had been greeted by his parents with ecstatic joy and unbridled celebration. Now, more grey than blonde, the diminutive widow was rapidly approaching her fiftieth year.

Robin was up early that day, having promised his mother a crayfish dinner for two that evening. The daily quota was four West Coast rock lobsters per licence, so a catch of four would provide a substantial meal.

The two boys had agreed the evening before that, weather permitting, they would rendezvous at their usual meeting point, a stone's throw from the beach used to launch the rubber ducks and rowing boats used by other prospectors in search of the local "kreef". They had a secret dive site known only to themselves. "Dillon's Spot", named after its discoverer, was located some one hundred metres off shore. But first they would meet, chat a bit about recent past and upcoming events and then kit up in preparation for the next two or three icy hours that lay ahead.

Unlike others of his age, Robin had not outgrown the habit of kissing his mother goodbye whenever he left her alone in the house, or was dropped off at some venue or another. His dive bag was permanently packed and ready to go, containing his full-length two-part wetsuit with hood, matching neoprene gloves and bootees, mask, snorkel, fins and finally his goody bag in which he would keep his catch of the day, crayfish measure and dive knife. The plastic measure was just to keep things legal in the size department and the knife, which he would later strap to his leg, was for "just in case".

The only piece of diving attire that didn't go into Robin's bag was his weight belt. Used to compensate for the buoyancy of his wetsuit, the weights were too heavy and cumbersome to be carried in the dive bag, so Robin routinely slung it around his waist and clasped it tight. The bag was then worn rucksack fashion on his back, with handles over shoulders, keeping arms and hands free for cycling.

Hugging his mother tight, Robin planted a kiss on her forehead, and then saddled up for the short ride to the beach.

"Bye!" shouted his mother after him. "Love you. Be careful!"

"You too, you too, you too," Robin replied, as he free-wheeled down the partially eroded gravel driveway and onto the Kommetjie Road. It was his standard response to her standard farewell.

It was still early morning, but the day was promising to be a real beauty, with wispy, pale candyfloss clouds way out to sea and the sun beginning to warm to the task ahead. Robin built up a slight sweat below his eyes and there was no cooling wind to blow through his wild blond curls. Not long, but curling down to just below his ear lobes, his unruly, rarely combed hair had earned him the unimaginative nickname of "Goldilocks", since the age of twelve. It had also earned his mother more than a few memos and code of conduct reminders from the high-school principal.

Robin chained his bike securely to his usual hitching post, a row of seven old concrete bollards with a rusty horizontal steel pipe running through the top of the first five. The two missing sections of pipe had been swallowed up by the elements and the remainder looked set to follow suit. He had often wondered why the bollards were there at all, protecting nothing and some twenty metres from the nearest pedestrian path and no road in sight. Still, it was a perfect place to park their bikes, leaving only their dive bags exposed to the threat of theft.

Whilst Robin was waiting for his friend to arrive, Shirley was at home doing what she always did on a Saturday morning …

laundry, dishes and little weeding of her herb garden for relaxation. She cut some basil to make a pesto for that evening and a small bunch of rocket to make herself a light salad for lunch. Returning through the back door and scullery to the kitchen, she experienced a sense of uneasiness and foreboding. She unplugged her cell phone from the charger and dialled her son's number. She waited a second or two for an answer, but was physically startled as the shrill ring tone of her son's phone sounded less than a metre from her ear. He had left it on a shelf in the kitchen, where he always left it when he went diving. Shirley knew that he never took his phone with him and berated herself for being so absent-minded and neurotic.

She took two small dice from a little red leather container attached to her car keys. They were a novelty Christmas cracker trinket from the previous year. Although she didn't consider herself to be a superstitious person, the dice were minor decision-makers in her life. A combined score of six or more invariably meant she would open a bottle of wine, do her shopping another day, or perform some other insignificant self-rewarding activity. Less than six and she would do the converse. As she rolled the dice in the palm of her hand, she determined that a score of six or less and she would drive down to the beach, just to make sure everything was as it should be with the boys. Her first roll resulted in one die landing on the floor, so that didn't count. With both dice rolled for the second time on the breakfast table, a pair of twos was not what she wanted to see. The "best of three" decision gave her a five and a two, followed by two fours; so all was well in the world.

Robin waited for almost an hour for his friend to arrive and with no phone at hand, the only way to find out what had happened to Dillon would be to cycle all the way to Misty Cliffs and back, which would take him almost an hour, what with his dive bag to carry. Unlike his mother, he didn't have a pair of decision-making dice, but he did have a "yes/no" coin (a stocking filler from that same Christmas) and his mother's compulsion to make decisions on the basis of a coin toss … or roll of the dice.

Robin had been diving for as long as he could recall. As a toddler, he would pull a pair of swimming goggles over his face and crawl amongst the rock pools. As a sixteenth birthday present, his mother had bought him scuba-diving lessons and, with the aid of some second-hand equipment, he had gained his open-water scuba-diving certificate. So Robin was fully aware of the golden rule of diving, that being to never dive alone. Although he had always obeyed the rules and was instinctively a cautious diver, whenever he and Dillon went crayfishing, they were seldom in a position whereby one "buddy" could assist another in need. Although they would always dive together in the same location, synchronised diving it was not.

Retrieved from a zipped pocket in his dive bag, a coin would determine if it would be "Yes, just take a look and see", or "No, just get back on your bike and go home".

The coin spun high and fell onto the coarse sandy beach. It embedded itself at a slight angle with one third buried, but left enough visible to tell Robin what the coin gods had decided. He accepted the "Yes" with about the same resignation that his mother had accepted her pair of twos and a best of three was similarly called for.

A "No" followed by the definitive "Yes" had Robin unzipping his dive bag and donning his wetsuit bottoms and overlapping jacket. Dillon's non-appearance had the young man slightly flustered and his normally routine pre-dive preparation became hurried and careless. He sat on broken shells and stones and pulled on his rubber-soled bootees. He felt the sun slowly baking him in his jet-black wetsuit and sweat rolled down his cheeks and the small of his back. His diving knife was strapped to the inside of his calf – not the outside, where it could snare on a tube of kelp. The goody bag was secured and his weight belt swung around his hips, hitched up to his waist and buckled fast.

Shirley was startled by the sound of her back door slamming shut, as a sudden breath of wind toyed with her nerves. She stopped her garlic-crushing pesto preparation and gingerly stepped into the scullery. The door was opened again and a basket full of vegetables would keep it so, regardless of any amount of wind. That feeling of unease had not dissipated and Shirley was not fully concentrating on the task at hand, albeit a simple task that would not normally be considered demanding.

A rustling sound emanating from within her scullery had Shirley replacing the garlic crusher in her right hand with a carving knife from the wooden block, that held an assortment of kitchen knives and was within easy reach. She gripped it firmly, as one would grip to stab, and slowly took one step towards the open door that separated scullery from kitchen. Four more steps and she would be able to see if anyone or anything was in or around her house.

Robin waded into the icy water until waist deep, and then took his mask, fins and gloves from the goody bag. He was skilled in slipping a fin over one foot, whilst half squatting on the other leg and maintaining balance against the gently breaking wash of the sea, then repeating the action for the other fin. First left then right. He didn't know why, but it was always in that order. His dive mask and attached snorkel were stretched into place like a headband, but not pulled down over his eyes, and gloves snapped tight over tingling blue fingers … first left and then right.

He lay on his back and kicked his way out through the inner forest of kelp, glancing over his shoulder for a natural passage or slightly easier path through the wrinkled frons of seaweed, with their lasagna texture and dark brown hue. Only once he was beyond the visible clutches of the weed did Robin remove his mask and snorkel and pull his hoody over his ears and forehead, carefully tucking away stray locks that invariably resisted being hidden. Spitting a couple of times into each lens of his mask before rinsing it would ensure that they remained mist free and clear to see all creatures great and small.

Robin dipped his head under water, coughed high the few drops of water hiding in the snorkel and with arms by his side, kicked his way out to "the spot", the whereabouts of which he instinctively knew. It was a good ten-minute swim, through small rolling, unrelenting waves that were no obstacle to the fit young man. Occasionally, he would stop and tread water, only to catch his breath and take a four-point bearing from the lighthouse, mountainside church and two distinctive-looking houses, which the former two landmarks were required to obscure, in order that his destination be reached.

When he was satisfied that he had reached the required distance out to sea and the designated buildings had moved into their correct location, Robin turned and paused to take in the view. One moment it was nothing but sea and sky, the next a landscape of pure beauty … a hundred or so tiny Kommetjie homesteads, impressive mountains of pure green or fire-ravished grey, dots of people walking the beaches and Noordhoek, way off in the distance ... a moment to capture it all, before the next wave rolled by and snatched it from him.

Taking deep breaths of the salty air, Robin filled his lungs, held then released ... in, out, in ... out. Hyperventilating his lungs initiated a little light-headedness at first, but enriched his blood with excess oxygen and, if controlled sensibly, did his body no harm. One final deep breath and Robin plunged headlong into the depths, descending rapidly to the bottom of the sea, which was about twelve metres deep in this particular spot. Isolated strands of kelp came up to greet him, some of which he used to steady himself against the surge of the sea. The sea bed was a mass of rocky outcrops upon which only the strongest of seaweed tendrons were capable of attaching themselves, limpet-like, becoming one with their granite host. Cape gale-force winds and unrelenting winter swells left most of the rocks this far out from the beach relatively barren and bare, but there was enough kelp to be of some assistance to a determined diver.

Gripping the foot of one such tube of kelp with one hand, Robin eased his way forward, peering down and over a particularly promising overhang. Where the rock protruded from the sandy sea bed, a small inlet gave shelter to a multitude of sea life. As the sand was washed gently to and fro, Robin could see three or four pairs of long, fine red antennae sifting their way through small puffs of sand clouds. A small pyjama shark eased its way through the swell, following the contours of the rock between diver and sand.

Having located the spot, Robin returned to the surface for fresh air. A few seconds to replenish his lungs and he was hovering above his unsuspecting prey once more. He was well practiced and quick, grabbing one of the creatures as far back along the body as he could reach. At the first hint of danger, crayfish retreated deep into their lairs, locking themselves into crevices with spiky armour-plated legs. Robin shook his catch violently, loosening the kreef's grip and returned to the surface with the catch firmly in hand. Treading water, he measured the crayfish and then stuffed it into his blue goody bag, satisfied that it was of legal size and not a female in berry. One down, three to go.

As Shirley peered around the doorframe, the back door slammed shut once more. The vegetable basket doorstop was gone and the telltale hairs on the back of her neck were sending out their warning. A shiver travelled down her back as her thoughts immediately turned to the front door, left open to encourage a little fresh air to circulate through the house. She briskly walked to the door, looking all about her in the process … to see what she might not wish to see. Should she lock the door, or maybe just run as fast as she could down the lane to the main road? There were cars travelling that road continuously, so that would surely mean safety. Weighing up her options in a fraction of a second, she decided that the least favourable alternative was to be trapped in her own house, with an outsider determined to enter.

Leaving the front door open and looking left and right as if crossing heavy traffic, she took the first tentative steps into daylight. The driveway lay before her. She turned to face the house and, taking minute steps, retreated back some ten metres, seeing more and more of the rear garden as she went. Curiosity was eating away at the fright within. Given enough distance between her and whoever the intruder was outside her back door, she would still be able to reach the relative safety of the main road in the event of an ensuing chase. Moving in a slow, deliberate arc towards the mountain, but slightly away from her house, Shirley edged her way back up the hill, determined to expose the intruder's whereabouts.

Meanwhile, Robin had bagged three decent-sized crayfish and was preparing for what he hoped would be his last dive of the day. He had been diving on and off for well over an hour and exhaustion was becoming a factor. Ever-decreasing "bottom time" and longer periods of rest on the surface were indications that his body was taking strain. The sun glistened off the top of the water and his face was feeling salty and sunburnt. Wallowing on his back and just gently fanning his arms below his body, he drew deeply on the air for one final plunge. He had combed the area pretty thoroughly and, on his last decent, had spotted a likely looking crack in the top surface of a solitary boulder, which was about three metres long. It was easily accessible and numerous antennae were flicking and frisking the water above.

The large rock was rounded like a giant Easter egg, cracked open along its length by eager little hands in search of chocolate button contents. The rock offered nothing to hold onto, but Robin had predetermined to anchor himself with a clenched fist within the crevice, as a mountaineer would do on a rock face. It was to be a quick smash and grab. Robin dived, kicked and thrust his hand into the crack, formed a fist and locked himself against the surge of the sea. Inches away and as yet undisturbed, two enormous antenna protruded from the split in the rock. Robin attacked, sinking his hand deep into the abyss. He had the crayfish, but his grip was not ideal. If he pulled or shook now, the base of the antennae and perhaps a few legs would surely snap off, freeing his dinner. He inched his hand in deeper and further along the body of the animal, which was by now pinned back as far as it could retreat. Satisfied he had bagged his quota, he shook and then pulled his hand from the crack.

Robin's hand was emerging … He could see the flesh of his wrist, the flesh that should have been covered by a neoprene glove. In pulling his hand from within, his glove had rolled up neatly to the widest part of his hand … where it had stuck. Unable to retreat further, the glove formed a perfect seal between body and granite.

A thousand and one thoughts flashed through the boy's mind in a second. He had always rolled his wetsuit sleeve over his gloves for that very reason. Why had he not done so this time? He didn't have time to ponder the ifs and buts of earlier actions. He must stay calm and not think about his lungs, which would soon be pounding out their message like jungle drums of doom. The crayfish was released in an instant, as was Robin's deliberately anchored fist. He would re-insert his right hand and then place his left hand beside it, as if praying…which clearly he was now doing.

His middle finger inched down the tendons and bright blue veins of his wrist, but not far enough. There was insufficient room to get his rescue hand in further, but he had to. He thrust his hand deeper but, being gloved, it was just too large for the available space. He hadn't time to remove the glove from his left hand, nor did he know how too, except with his teeth. There just wasn't time for that.

A couple of bubbles involuntarily escaped from the side of his mouth, as if reason and calmness were being discharged from his inner being. One last attempt to claw back the neoprene bangle was aborted as sheer terror instinctively took over the situation. Robin jerked and pulled back and forth as little scratches on the back of his hand leaked oxygen-depleted blood into the water.

On the surface, tiny bubbles were lost as a rogue wave broke into a million foaming fragments, before returning the area to a serine and tranquil seascape.

As the last of the larger bubbles burst and mingled with the fresh air, Shirley had found sufficient courage to edge her way to the diamond-mesh fence, that patrolled the perimeter of their property.

A solitary juvenile baboon was devouring the little that remained of her vegetables. The basket had been discarded, as had her dustbin. Newspapers, empty tins and plastic bottles littered the area. It was an utter mess, but Shirley neither minded, nor cared. A baboon, she thought, just a bloody baboon … all that worrying for nothing. Soon Robin would be home and they would feast on crayfish, mayonnaise mixed with pesto and a fresh ciabatta soaked in olive oil. What could be better than that?

SPLIT SECOND

Pearl had been with the practice for almost thirty years, during which time she'd seen doctors come and go, accounted for their books and diarised their appointments.

The oak panel door opened and she poked her purple hair, button nose and spectacles into view.

"Mrs Scott is waiting for you, doctor. Shall I show her in?"

Dr Williams looked up from his desk and set his pen to one side. He walked towards the door, ready to greet his next forty-five-minute appointment.

Linda Scott was in her late forties and looked every bit that age. Five months ago she'd have been given the benefit of the doubt, had she claimed to be just turning forty. Jonathan Williams had ceased with formalities, as had she several sessions ago, at about the same time he'd stopped asking if she took milk and sugar with her coffee.

"Linda! How are you? You are looking radiant," he lied.

"Coffee?" He added, not waiting for her answer. She always had a coffee and he always said that he wouldn't join her.

"If I had a cup of coffee with every appointment, I'd be wired to the moon by lunchtime." It was their little opener and he was careful to call her an "appointment" and not a "patient".

He poured the coffee, added a touch of milk, but caught the sugar spoon on the edge of the coffee cup, giving an even sprinkling of sugar to the top of the teak dresser. He wanted to say "shit" but said nothing. Pearl would sort out the mess later. He gingerly walked the coffee several paces across the plush thick-pile carpet to where Linda had seated herself in the large brown leather visitor's armchair. There was a traditional couch propping up the far wall, but that was currently being used as storage space for a volume of medical journals and his golf clubs, which didn't fit into the boot of his car. It was Wednesday and he was teeing off at two-twenty that afternoon.

"I remember a dinner some months ago," he said, placing the coffee before the diminutive Mrs Scott. Divorced and not unattractive, but with a skin tone that cried out for a few days of sunshine and hair that urgently needed the attention of a stylist, she was not the doctor's type. "The hostess had one of those filter coffee makers, but the plunger variety." Linda nodded as best she could, whilst taking her first sip of the steaming drink and, unsure if it was too hot for another, she held it hovering above the saucer.

"I know the sort."

"Well, as she pushed it down, the whole thing exploded … shattered into a million tiny pieces. There was glass and hot coffee everywhere. It completely ruined her evening and although a band aid was sufficient for a small cut to her finger, the real damage was done."

A little small talk was the usual prelude to a session with Dr Williams.

"Funny thing is, no matter how much everyone tried to convince her it was an accident, my hostess convinced herself even more that it wasn't. She said she'd plunged it too hard, or maybe the glass jug was too cold for the boiling water. We all knew it wasn't that. Most probably a rogue bubble in the glass or a hairline crack somewhere … bubbles and hairline cracks, maybe."

"I see you don't use one," said Linda, casting a glance towards the dresser and the still steaming percolator.

"That's the funny thing. I knew it was a one-in-a-thousand-chance accident, but I still wouldn't dream of using one … not at home, or here at work. Silly, don't you think?"

There was a raised seam at the end of the leather chair's arm rest, either side of which brass studs dug the leather deep into the framework beneath. Linda was nervously plucking at the seam with the bitten fingernail of her thumb, whilst simultaneously biting what was left of her other nails, as if it were her last supper.

Her eyes were wild and transfixed … her fist pushed back the tip of her nose as she gnawed at a piece of loose cuticle.

"Linda?" enquired Jonathan, encouraging her to begin what she had come for, rather than prompt her to cease torturing his furniture and her fingertips.

"Would you like to carry on from last week, or maybe talk about something else completely? It's up to you … whatever you are comfortable with."

Jonathan knew her story. He'd heard about it the day it had happened. Read about the mother with the French-sounding name in the local newspaper twenty-four hours later. He'd listened to her GP describe it to him over the phone and then, two weeks after that, heard first hand from the woman now sitting in front of him. He knew about that moment, that instant when she was transformed from a rational, carefree woman at peace with the world, into a deranged, illogical, screaming being, incapable of thought or deed.

He had heard her explain how she had seen nothing that day, nothing but a flash of white from the left – a streak of white on the periphery of her vision … the hint of pink, she felt moments later, as it disappeared beneath the bonnet of her car. A dog … please god, let it be a dog.

"I didn't see her, Jonathan. I just didn't see her."

It would have been easy for him to hold her and tell her it wasn't her fault, but that was the way of friends and those close to the victim. Linda was a victim … a victim of her own self-guilt. She didn't need him to say, "Don't blame yourself."

Blame, guilt, fault; only she would finally be able to cast off the weight that was pulling her down into the deepest depths of despair. He was there to help her pick the lock that held the heavy iron chain of guilt tight around her neck. One day it will happen, but not today … one day.

"You know when you are driving and there is an ice-cream van further up the road," she said, plucking at the chair with increased vigour, "we instinctively slow the car right down. You know, just in case. We all do that, don't we?"

"But you weren't speeding, Linda. Everyone confirmed that – even the coroner."

"But not ice-cream van slow … not that slow. Why don't we all drive ice-cream van slow?" she said, voice cracking and tears welling up in her dark, sleep deprived, lifeless eyes.

"One second, maybe two seconds … it all comes down to seconds," said Jonathan. "A second slower and it would have been just the same, and you would still be sitting in that chair. It wasn't the speed. It wasn't anything that you, or I, or anyone else can explain. It just happened."

In one previous session, Linda had gone beyond the initial impact; that bump and the feeling of tangled flesh acting as brake between wheel and steel. She had described that instinctive feeling of knowing it wasn't a dog and how she sat in her stationary car for a brief moment – stuck in time, frozen in an event that would shape the remainder of so many lives. Mrs Bernaudon deprived of her only child, four grieving grandparents and a tiny white coffin carried by two uncles. Linda had watched the funeral from a criminal's vantage point, peering through the curtains of a small coffee shop across the road from St Joseph's Church.

The tears always helped. Linda stopped her armchair picking and took refuge in a deep breath and a cigarette. The reception desk "No Smoking" sign was plain to see, but Jonathan always had an ashtray handy in his office for Linda. She flicked a Camel from its soft packaging with her thumb, and lit it with the fifth strike of her lighter. Jonathan didn't mind Linda's habitual puff, as it was always pretty short-lived. She took one long, heavy drag and immediately stubbed out the fledgling fag, leaving her raw fingertips grey with ash, as she first stabbed, then squashed the extinguished Camel into submission.

"When I eventually got out of the car, the mother was kneeling on the pavement. She screamed a scream I never believed could come from a person. It was a wounded animal sound. I also screamed, but nothing came out. I screamed so loud in my head that I thought my skull would crack."

Jonathan pulled his chair as close as he could to his desk. He leaned forward and listened intently.

"They say you shouldn't move anyone who's been in an accident, but we had to. She was a twisted, mangled mess of white-and-red rags. Her leg was protruding between mud guard and wheel at a sickening, unnatural angle. I remember a tiny jagged bone sticking out where her shin should have been."

Jonathan recalled that two young men and an elderly gentleman had somehow found the strength to lift Linda's car sufficiently for a woman to drag the tiny, limp body from under the front axle of the vehicle. The mother whimpered inaudibly, rocking back and forth, partly shielding her eyes from the sight that seconds earlier, had been her precious little girl skipping down the high street.

"I didn't see her, Jonathan."

Dr Wlliams walked behind his patient, reaching around the leather back rest. He placed a hand on each shoulder.

"These things happen, Linda. They are nobody's fault. They just happen. It'll take time, but it will eventually get easier, I promise. How are you sleeping now? Are those tablets helping?" Jonathan's voice was gentle, yet firm and there was a sense of belief in the words he spoke. She needed those words ... needed them like a weekly fix. They made her feel alive again. She needed to come and be reassured. It was a quick forty-five-minute fix that would see her through the remainder of the week and partly into the next.

Linda rose from the comfort of her therapist's chair. Jonathan took her hands in his, as would a Pope with a sinner.

"Please remember, any time you feel you need to talk … and I mean anytime. Don't hesitate."

Dr Williams closed the door behind Mrs Scott and walked to the window behind his desk. Looking down onto the street below, Linda came into view. She stepped off the kerb between two cars parked back to front either side of her. She gently placed her fingertips on the bonnet of one and boot of the other.

She looked this way and that … searching, waiting, easing her head forward beyond the line of parked cars, but with her body withdrawn and protected from a possible passing glancing blow.

"Go on, Linda, cross the road, cross it. There's nothing coming. Cross the bloody road, Linda."

Her head turned from left to right, not once or twice, but eight, nine or ten times. She eventually obliged her doctor, secretly looking down on her and made the six-metre dash across the road to her car, parked in the relative safety of the far side.

Jonathan stepped back as Pearl opened the door once more. She was here to clear away cups, spilt sugar and liberally spray air fresher around the room. The doctor walked towards the door and caught his thigh a blow on the corner of his desk. He thought nothing but said "shit". Pearl had heard it all before.

"Mrs Bernaudon phoned to ask if we could change the day of her regular appointment. I said that I would check with you, but didn't think it would be a problem."

"No problem at all, Pearl. No, prob … unless of course, if she wants to book a Wednesday morning slot," he added, forgetting the pain in his thigh and pausing to take a practice swing with his imaginary three iron. He held the pose and turned towards his secretary.

"Perfect drive, Pearl, perfect drive. Straight down the middle."

THE DOOR

Lansdown Cricket Club was the epicentre of Harry's life in his late teens and early twenties. Seldom did a weekend pass without him practising in the nets on Friday evening, playing two cricket matches and waking up with three consecutive hangovers. His was a close-knit group of friends and team mates, all of whom were a few years older than Harry, whom they treated as a cherished younger brother. There was Duncan, Jenks and Tree, the latter being so named due to his six foot eight inches in stature. Not that Harry or the two others were lacking in height. Harry at six foot, Jenks a little taller and Duncan at six foot four and a bit, combined with Tree to make a conspicuous gang of four at the club.

Several of the members of the club lived in close proximity to the beautiful cricket ground, which was bounded by an orchard, a hospital, a publishing company and an avenue of four-storey detached Georgian houses, most of which were the temporary residence of doctors, nurses and a few hospital administrators.

No. 89 Cedric Road was the abode of Raymond Galley, the cricket club captain, whilst 93 was the property of the first XI wicketkeeper, Len Watkins. Harry, then in his first year out of school, lived with his mother and two sisters at No. 71 Cedric Road.

One rainy Saturday evening in June, when all but Duncan, Harry and the barman had left the club house, a plan was hatched from the depths of their beer glasses, that seemed both brilliant and side-splittingly funny. Bad weather had put an early end to the match and drinking had commenced in earnest as early as four o'clock in the afternoon. As the two plotted and drank, the hours rolled by and the storm outside grew teeth. The barman's patience had been more than stretched by 2.30 a.m. when he finally poured Harry and Duncan out of the door and secured the premises for the night.

Duncan piloted his Peugeot 325 with the sun roof open and Harry navigated as best he could, with the teeming rain and his long curly hair doing little to improve his already blurred vision. In five minutes they had reached the pick-up point. The two bedraggled accomplices staggered out of the idling car and fumbled their way to pile of concrete breeze blocks stacked neatly on the side of the road. The building site had been passed frequently by Duncan and was easy meat at that time of the morning. One by one the blocks were transferred from sodden site to equally sodden car boot. Cricket kit was flung to all parts of the car in an attempt to cram in just enough materials to render a return trip unnecessary. The getaway was clean and sweet, but laboured, as the Peugeot struggled to leave with its illicit cargo. At a time when common sense and lucid thoughts were rare commodities, Duncan finally closed the sun roof.

The two young men sat motionless in the Peugeot 325. In the half light of the street lamp outside No. 93 Cedric Road, their breathing was heavy and steam rose from their saturated cotton-clad torsos. It was decision time and neither Duncan nor Harry has any intention of returning the stolen blocks from whence they came. Len Watkins and his family had just left for their summer holidays, having recently completed some minor home improvements to their back garden. Len had been so proud of his newly constructed fishpond, pergola and crazy paving that he'd mentioned little else to his cordon of slip fielders in the preceding weeks of Somerset league cricket. All Duncan and Harry needed was just a touch of good fortune and a persistent storm to muffle the sounds of their sinister plot.

The touch of good luck was with them as Harry pointed to the open garage window, which was a convenient height and size to be entered with ease by the younger man. As Harry clambered ungainly through the garage window opening, he turned to his accomplice and grinned wryly. Duncan turned the knob of the adjacent garage door, only to find it unlocked. Both sniggered and simultaneously shushed each other with fingers to their lips. A wheelbarrow, trowel, a quarter of a bag of cement and a spade were removed from the garage. They half-filled the barrow with soil from the back garden and the contents of the cement bag were emptied enthusiastically on top. The torrential rain had continued throughout the operation and provided the third vital ingredient in sufficient quantity. The mortar mixture was prepared in just a few minutes.

Harry wheeled the barrow the few metres down the road to Ray Galley's house, where Duncan had parked his car. Concrete blocks were unloaded from the car and carefully carried to Galley's front door. All of the Cedric Road houses were of similar design, with a recessed front door set back from an opening in the external wall, which formed a porch, used by most residents to display pot plants of varying types. Galley's porch offered no such distractions. It was bare and quite clearly needed a little inspirational home improvement. Duncan and Harry knew exactly what was required. Duncan passed the blocks, as Harry dug deep into the barrow with the only trowel they had at their disposal. In very little time, they had erected a tidy block wall almost to waist height between the reveals of the porch opening. Harry extricated himself from within the newly created tomb and resumed work from the outside.

The last course of blockwork was awkward to lay and left a gap of a couple of inches between the top of the wall and underside of the opening. Nevertheless, with the aid of Duncan's extra height and some hand-packed mortar, the job was complete. After wiping down the wall with their bare wet hands to smoothen out the mortar oozing from between each course, the dynamic duo stood back in admiration for almost a minute, before cold and fatigue began to take toll. Duncan got behind the wheel of his car once more, leaving Harry to wheel his borrowed barrow home to No. 71 Cedric Road and sleep off the remainder of the night in his welcoming bed.

Little detective work was required of the policeman who greeted Harry's mother the following morning. A trail of cementitious sludge led from Len Watkins' place to Ray Galley's house and then on to No. 71 where a dirty wheelbarrow lay on its side in the driveway, testament to the night's mischievous capers. Galley had been awakened by his daughter who had been sent downstairs to fetch the Sunday papers and milk. The young girl had been more than slightly distressed to find a wall between her and the outside world and had returned to her parents' bedroom teary-eyed and very confused. The telltale trail had been followed by Galley some thirty minutes prior to the arrival of the officer he had summoned from the Somerset Constabulary. The policeman tried desperately to conceal his amusement by reminding himself that this was a total waste of the force's over-stretched resources.

Harry received the obligatory caution, but was far more concerned with the prospect of having to field for three hours with a monster hangover, during their Sunday fixture with rival Bath

Cricket Club. It was already a scorcher of a day, even by British standards.

Duncan was obviously nowhere to be found that Sunday morning, as Harry dismantled the wall block by block, scrubbed the reveals of the porch clean and returned any salvageable materials to their owners.

Harry scored a streaky four through the slips and dropped two catches that day, whilst Duncan took three wickets and made twelve runs from two mighty blows over long off.

Over the following days and weeks, the tale of "the bricking up of Galley's front door" was told and retold in bars and clubs around the Georgian City of Bath.

Galley never mentioned the episode again.

THE INTERVIEW

The motorway was baking under the relenting torture of the late-morning Western Cape sun, in sharp contrast to the air-conditioned interior of Peter Kilpin's cool blue Range Rover. The handful of vehicles ahead of him lead the way to the off-ramp that marked the end of the M1 to Muizenberg, not thirty minutes from the centre of Cape Town. Peter's destination was the building site where, if the main contractor was on programme, Kilpin Engineering would shortly be supplying and erecting the structural steel trusses for a small, but sustainable shopping centre in False Bay.

He tilted his can of diet Pepsi and, straw in mouth, probed for the last few droplets of liquid hiding in the bottom of the tin. The pepper-steak pie and soft drink would serve as lunch, but this fast-food diet was not helping his waistline. He pinched the ample portion of belly that was suffocating his belt and secretly vowed to settle for a small Greek salad that evening as penance.

The traffic lights at the top of the intersection conspired to halt his progress. To his left and no more than twenty metres down the road, he noticed a figure standing erect and still to one side of the dual carriageway. In the time it took the lights to change their mind and flash him a green arrow, Peter carefully studied the man, whose curly white peppercorn hair betrayed his age. The temperature gauge in Peter's car was hovering around the thirty-degrees mark, yet here stood a man who closely resembled Madiba, other than being dressed in a dark three-piece suit, white shirt and tie, as opposed to the obligatory loose-fitting multi-coloured silk shirt. Closer inspection revealed it to be a two-piece suit, worn over a dark front-buttoned sweater, which masqueraded as waistcoat. A trilby sat neatly on top of the slender tall man and the raincoat folded neatly over one arm gave the appearance of a 1950s' middle-class British bank manager from Bromley.

Clarence stood straight and still. He took a white handkerchief from the breast pocket of his jacket and dabbed the sweat from his brow. He rested his empty plastic lunch box on his raincoat arm and raised his trilby slightly, not as one may in deference to Mrs Jones who had recently transferred her account from Lloyds, but in order to mop his forehead a little more thoroughly and allow what breeze existed that day to pass between head and hat. Without lowering his head, he wiped a shoe on the back of his trouser leg – not that his already highly polished footwear needed the attention, but the occupant of the fancy 4x4 at the intersection would not be impressed with dusty brogues should he decide to stop. As with the military, Clarence did not allow himself the indignity of an outstretched arm and upturned thumb. A lift would be appreciated if offered, but he wasn't begging.

As Peter turned the corner and headed on his way, he glanced at the old man who didn't flinch, other than to return his lunch box hand to his side. Peter pulled over and switched on his hazard lights, though he'd previously ascertained there to be no traffic behind him. He looked back over his shoulder, expecting the old man to at least be making an effort to close the short gap between hitchhiker and lift. Peter reversed a little, wound down the passenger window and wound down his head.

"Like a lift anywhere?"

The man stooped low, opened the door and took his seat. "Thank you, sir," he said politely, as he folded his raincoat neatly on his lap.

"So where are you heading? Oh, and you may want to put this on," Peter said, tugging twice at his own seat belt, as would a pre-flight air hostess. The man's name was Clarence and he was heading for Simonstown, which was some distance past his own destination, and the roadworks between the one and the other made that particular route a tedious journey at times.

Another set of traffic lights brought a dishevelled-looking young boy to Peter's window, a pair of cupped outstretched hands ready to accept any small offering that may come his way. A single raised hand signalled Peter's reluctance to participate, however a disparaging look, muttered expletive and a green light were required before the boy took two steps back from the moving vehicle. Clarence tutted and shook his head, leaving Peter wondering whether the subject of his disapproval was disappearing into the background or seated behind the wheel of a cool blue Range Rover.

"Beggars, sir ... too many beggars," cleared up that matter, as Clarence continued to shake his head.

"Yes, they're everywhere ... and if you give to them once, you only encourage them the next time. Oh, and it's Peter, not sir."

"Yes sir, Peter, sir," repeated the old man.

"Listen, Clarence, I'm only going as far as Muizenberg, which is just up the road, so I'll have to drop you off there and you can catch the train the rest of the way," said Peter, turning to his passenger for approval at the suggestion.

"Thank you sir...that will be fine. You are very kind. I'll walk from there."

"Walk? To Simonstown?" asked Peter incredulously. "It will take you forever – you can't do that."

As Clarence explained that he walked almost everywhere rather than pay the exorbitant train or township taxi fares, Peter listened intently. And when the old man revealed that he'd left at three o'clock that same morning to be in Simonstown eleven hours later, Peter did metal gymnastics to try to calculate the average walking speed necessitated by such a journey, but gave up not knowing exactly where Blue Downs was situated within the mass of sprawling townships, which dominated the Cape Flats.

"Was that your breakfast?" asked Peter, glancing down at the empty plastic box, as he eased a silent pie-and-Pepsi belch from the window side of his mouth.

"Breakfast, lunch and supper," replied the passenger.

As they approached Muizenberg, Clarence made clear the purpose of his journey. His host wriggled a little uncomfortably in his leather seat as a tale of abject poverty and destitution unfolded. Peter knew of the suffering on the Cape Flats and a thousand other such areas throughout South Africa, but found himself unsettled to hear first-hand the account of an old man, who lived in a corrugated-iron shack with his two daughters, son-in-law and three grandchildren. There was no weekly income in Clarence's shack, but plenty of mouths to feed every day. His wife had passed away last year and his daughters could find no work. His eldest daughter Mary was beaten by her "no good husband" whose life of petty crime and pushing drugs in the suburbs fuelled his thirst for cheap brandy. Yet here was a man well past his prime, dressed neatly in his "Sunday best" with perfectly pressed trousers and hand-stitched brown leather elbow patches to give an extra year or two of life to his precious solitary jacket.

The Range Rover eased through Muizenberg and beyond his shopping centre building site, which Peter decided could as easily be visited on the way back from Simonstown. Clarence seemed oblivious to the fact that his driver was travelling further than either of them had expected.

"And why Simonstown?" enquired Peter eventually. "I haven't even asked you why you are going to Simonstown."

"I have an interview there this afternoon at three o'clock," explained Clarence.

"Then you'll be a bit early … And an interview for what … with whom?"

Clarence revealed that he had applied for a job as a caretaker to the Admiral, who resided at the naval base in Simonstown. He produced an envelope from inside his jacket pocket, explaining that it contained confirmation of his appointment with the Admiral's secretary. He offered it to "Sir" to read, but Peter declined; not only because he was driving, but he had little doubt that the envelope contained the cherished letter, as stated.

A couple of yachts were out motor sailing in the gentle breeze between the swing moorings just outside the harbour. The road followed the railway line, which in turn followed the coastline. As they approached Simonstown railway station, Clarence requested to be dropped off as he intended spending the two and half hours of newly acquired spare time sitting on one of the several public benches provided on the beach promenade. The beach and station were close neighbours and shared the comforting shade of a small cluster of tall blue gum trees.

Peter pulled the car over outside the railway station and Clarence stepped outside. "Goodbyes" and "thanks" were exchanged for "good lucks" and a "don't mention it" as Clarence closed the door and Peter indicated his intention to re-join the light traffic. Peter kept his car in neutral, switched off his indicator and unbuckled his seat. Lifting his bum from the seat, he took out his wallet and extracted a hundred rand note. Clarence was ambling slowly towards the beach lane, so it took little more than a call through an open car window to turn him back.

"Here, Clarence, take this … Maybe you can buy something for lunch," said Peter, as he stretched across the passenger seat and offered the note through the open window.

"No, sir, I couldn't … You are too kind," replied the old man, whose reluctant words were not matched by the swiftness of his hands, which although not grabbing, were pleased to be in receipt of the donation.

Clarence stood this time and watched as Peter made a U-turn and headed back towards his original destination. He offered a half-hearted wave with the note in his hand and watched his benefactor drive away. He the placed his raincoat between his knees, Tupperware on the pavement and once more reached inside his jacket pocket for the envelope. Opening it, he carefully deposited his one-hundred-rand note inside, where it joined three notes of similar denomination, as well as a single fifty.

Clarence returned the envelope to its pocket and crossed the main road, where he stood patiently for about ten minutes, standing erect, tall and as proud as an on-duty guard outside Buckingham Palace. Eight or nine cars went by before the next one slowed and stopped.

He opened the door and once more sat in the air-conditioned comfort of a luxury car.

"Hello there, I'm Hans. Where are you going?" asked the new arrival, as he accelerated out of Simonstown.

"Peter, sir. The name is Peter and I'm heading for Cape Town, where I have an interview for a job as caretaker for Vodacom."

"Vodacom, eh? Well good luck with that, but I can only take you as far as Claremont."

"Thank you, sir … that will be fine. You are very kind. I'll walk from there." With those words, he took an envelope from his jacket and offered it to the driver, to read the contents. His driver declined – they always did. He just hoped that this one wouldn't leave him ambling on the pavement for quite so long before reaching for his wallet. After all, he was no beggar. He'd never asked anything of anyone and he never would. The car was cool, the ride was smooth and he'd probably be in Cape Town within forty-five minutes. What a fine day it was turning out to be.

THE THIRD PEA

A filtered, comforting warmth awoke the first awareness of being within the seed. The seed, which was within the pod, upon the stem and in the garden. There was nothing more, nor need there be. A protective pod of silky inner softness and the penetrating gentle heat, which provided nearly everything a fledgling pea could desire. A near constant flow of sweet liquid sustenance and the ever-present, all-consuming greenness of it all. The tiny pea was content, but tired. It had after all, been an extremely long and exhausting first awakening.

Early life was routine and simple, evenly divided into two distinctive periods. There were either interludes of warm, bright green light, or dark olive, almost black periods of existence, during which the warmth evaporated and was replaced by a chill that was only just bearable.

As the pea soaked up the life-giving liquid and bathed in the glow of the day, it grew steadily stronger. It felt more aware, more perceptive and acutely conscious of being in the presence of other similar beings. Then there were the sounds that filtered through the pod; strange sounds and in ever-increasing variety and volume.

Some of these noises evoked new feelings within; feelings of fear, anxiety and uncertainty. Although the pod was still there to defend, there seemed to be a greater force beyond its bright green protective shield. As the pea developed, the pod stretched and gave way subserviently to the expanding inner strength of its tenant, which was by now, almost the size of a small pea.

Before too long, the pod could not conceal the fact that the pea was not alone in its comforting cocoon. There were other peas, with obvious similarities, although not all equally formed.

Communication was instinctive and telepathic, having evolved through millennia; the pea and others like it had long since declined the more rudimentary path of primitive contact offered by nature and so eagerly adopted by primates and other species incapable of vegetative thought transmission (VTT). By projecting the right questions, it was soon established that there were seven inhabitants of the pod. Two slightly smaller peas existed in that direction and four more peas the other way. The third pea was elated that fate had dealt it a pretty good hand, not being one of the small ones on the end. Being an "end pea" had serious drawbacks. Not only was there the single-neighbour status to contend with, but given the pod's propensity to expand mainly from the middle, the end peas were constrained in growth and showed signs of seriously inhibited development.

Despite minor inequalities and petty differences of opinion, arising mainly from the increasingly important issue of spatial awareness, the peas generally got on with one another, inventing games and pretending not to know what the fifth pea has implied about the second, nor which pea was taking more than its fair share of liquid flowing through the spine of the pod. Every now and again that liquid appeared to be enriched with a mind-spinning goodness, an additive of sorts that had given them all an euphoric out-of-pod experience, albeit temporary and with an equally potent feeling of depression after the glow had dissipated. How they yearned for that special mixture and no sooner had they received it, they craved more, each pea forgetting the pledge not to over-indulge and deny a neighbour some of their life-giving entitlement.

Although never short of thoughts to exchange or games to play, they all concurred that "eye spy with my little eye" had long ceased to be an enjoyable pastime, especially since the banning of the letters "g" and "p" from further use.

By mutual consent, they had each been allocated a name; and so it was that "first pea", "second pea", "third pea", "Geoff", "fifth pea", "Greenie" and "Phnung" acquired their identities. The third pea was pleased with the name, as it conveyed a certain status – equal to the first pea in all but name.

Life for the average pea wasn't all fun and games. Geoff and the third pea would often debate the meaning of their existence. Was there life after this? What did it all mean? Was their pod the only true pod, or were there other, more powerful pods? Geoff had even suggested that there may be an alternative life form beyond theirs. How the others all laughed at that one. Greenie implied that Geoff had been indulging in more than his fair share of the good stuff and "where did he get it, because they'd all like some?" As the jibes abated, the third pea pondered Geoff's theory. Imagine that; another world outside this one … maybe it wasn't such a ridiculous concept.

During one period of dark greenness, the third pea was awakened by an unfamiliar sound, which appeared to be emanating from beyond their pod. The rasping, grating sound grew with gradual intensity throughout the dark and into the first shafts of light green, with an unrelenting, methodical and almost hypnotic regularity. The warm soft green light that had always offered comfort now revealed the dark grey silhouette of something sinister. The crunching, crushing, gnawing noise was out there, but seemed to be getting closer, pausing occasionally, only to recommence with increased voracity.

The dark grey grew darker as the silhouette devoured the last thin piece of membrane that was once their guardian, their home and their life. A hideous, rubbery creature with corrugated skin and devoid of any definition appeared, as it twisted this way and that … arching, contorting and extending its molten form into their inner sanctuary. Two tiny black spots flanked a serrated opening through which it had consumed all in its path.

Poised above the third pea as if to strike, the creature lurched to one side, attaching itself to the helpless and hapless Geoff. The third pea felt the desperate cries of a friend in need, but could do nothing to change the inevitable course of Geoff's destiny. Frothy cuckoo spit slime encircled the insatiable opening, as it melted deep into the flesh of the third pea's neighbour.

Without warning, the pod shook violently, more than it had shaken on a few previous occasions, when they'd heard the rhythmic sounds that swayed them back and forth for what seemed an eternity. In an instant, the creature was dragged by some mighty force, back through the hole in the pod, carrying with it a sizeable piece of its prey. Once gone, a blinding light filled the space vacated by the beast. It lit up the pod with intensity so great that the third pea had to constrain the instinctive compulsion to investigate further.

The other peas were abuzz with excitement, urging the third pea to relate what had just transpired. There was a hole in the pod. Yes, they all understood that, but what was beyond that hole? The third pea could not describe the scene outside, as there was no way to describe "blue" to beings that knew nothing but various shades of "green". They were less than satisfied with "not much really, but a different sort of not much" and they pressed the third pea for more. It was only then that the third pea realised that a familiar thought was missing from the clamour of thoughts bouncing around the pod. Geoff was silent.

A large piece of flesh was missing from the body closest to the third pea and with the passing of Geoff, a large piece of the third pea's life was missing. Silence ruled the pod, as the reality set in. They were no longer "the magnificent seven", as Phnung often referred to them. They were now six and life in the pod would never be the same.

Dark greens came and went, interspersed with light greens, but now they had a small patch of blue, which occasionally allowed a blinding, intense light to enter, bringing added warmth to the inhabitants of the pod. The six peas grew ever bigger and stronger, whilst the body of Geoff remained where it had been savaged. Now slightly wrinkled and withered, it was turning an unpleasant shade of dark green, not dissimilar to the colour of the life-sapping creature. The third pea was comforted in the belief that the creature had paid the ultimate price for its attack on Geoff. Maybe Geoff was now living that life beyond the pod, with other beings. Maybe the other beings were … blue. There was no other pea with whom the third pea could share such thoughts. The others just didn't understand.

Only one thing was certain. The third pea really missed Geoff.

A sudden surge of chemically enriched liquid nutrients temporarily distracted the third pea from a bout of severe depression. Later, that depression returned, intensified by the thought that the six were now growing stronger and fatter, due partly to the fact that their share of liquid was now even greater. The third pea turned disturbed thoughts of guilt back to thoughts of Geoff, now a shrivelled husk, a decayed reminder of an old friend.

Early one light green, just as the brightness was rising, the lives of the magnificent six (as the second pea now referred to them – much to the chagrin of the third pea) were irrevocably changed. The shaking had returned … the shaking that had preempted the arrival of the creature snatcher. But this shaking was more violent and more sustained. No thoughts were exchanged, as the peas awaited the outcome of these terrifying tremours. Sudden feelings of euphoria and elation were instantly replaced by an almighty thump as the entire pod appeared to be projected through space at incredible speed and then instantly halted.

Having survived the landing, the third pea was suddenly bombarded with questions from the others, wanting to know what was outside, through the hole and beyond the pod. The crash was of such force that the pod had slightly spilt along the seam. Weakened by the previously formed hole, the pod had neatly separated exactly between the third pea and Geoff's carcass. It revealed a sea of green objects, some of which were completely open, others firmly closed. The third pea could clearly make out the forms of other peas and pods. Some peas lay within half an opened pod, with obvious gaps where other peas should be. Then there were individual, pod-less peas, cast out of their homes by some being. Perhaps that being was the same one that had been moments too late to save Geoff.

Time passed, but not in the manner that the third pea was used to. The light no longer brought with it that warmth and the dark no longer cold. There was no gentle swaying, nor pitter-patter on the pod. Gone too was that zest for life they'd all had, the banter and the games. It wasn't about Geoff, as they'd enjoyed themselves as best they could even after Geoff had gone. There was something else missing; something they all yearned, no … craved. Where was their liquid, their life source, their life? They couldn't survive without it, especially the blend which gave such giddy pleasure and meaning to their existence. Now that it was gone, they wanted it, needed it even more.

Life in their pod, in the new place with other pods and orphaned peas, became a dreary, interminable, meaningless existence. Shared thoughts became infrequent, as energy was conserved and the will to communicate simply dried up, as had their precious juice. So this was it, thought the third pea. This is what it all amounts to. We come into this world, we live for a while and then something transports us and others like us to a place where we all starve to death. That's if we are lucky enough to survive being eaten alive by some rubbery, deformed creature.

As more time went by the third pea began to feel weak. A weakness borne of frustration and depression, rather than a physical inability to cope with the rigours of a post-pod-dependent life. Drifting in and out of conscious thought, the third pea would cast deep into memories of the early days with the others … days of fun, with Geoff and Greenie doing their infamous impressions of first pea and second pea pretending to be intellectually superior. Then there was Phnung's "knock-knock" joke, the punch line for which the third pea could never remember. Who's there? Something beginning with "g". No, that wasn't it.

As the third pea tried in vain to remember who was knocking and why, there was a very loud and distinctly real knock-knock from outside and, by the sound of it, this was no joke!

The slit in the pod had enlarged significantly as the pea's former protector and guardian had wilted and withered, starved of nutrition and deprived of natural light. Through the aperture, the third pea had gradually been able to see more and more of the surrounding landscape. They were all being held in some sort of receptacle. There were other peas and other creatures like peas, insofar as they were green, but at the same time there were things that were not green. Like the blue was not green, these were not green either … nor blue. It was most confusing, but intriguing, nevertheless.

The new source of the knocking was soon to be revealed. From the edge of the slit in the pod, a glimpse of a creature so vast left the third pea mesmerised and in awe. All thoughts of liquid evaporated as a long alien form with five stalk-like digits moved across the pile of pods, collecting a few at a time, before disappearing out of sight. The creature that killed Geoff was large, as must have been the creature that killed the creature that killed Geoff, but this new alien was on an unimaginable scale in comparison. Each time it returned it took more pods. There must have been as many as ten in one such grab. So massive was this alien that even when it came into full view, the third pea was incapable of determining where it ended. It was one very long alien, with five grabbers at one end.

Before long, the magnificent six and the body of Geoff were scooped up with others of their kind. Their pod was ripped apart without mercy and immediately two stalks plucked the second pea from the umbilical cord, that had been its life line for so long. The unfortunate pea disappeared upward and at great velocity, but the others could not determine its final destination, such was the speed of ascent and magnitude of the alien being before them. The first pea was similarly collected, but prematurely dropped from the pincer-like grip, plummeting into the abyss below. The remaining peas were piled on one another and contained in a small vessel, all naked, exposed and humiliated. It was a sickening sight. More and more peas followed a similar fate and before long, the third pea was starting to feel penned in and somewhat claustrophobic. Their pod had never imparted such a feeling upon its fledgling peas, although the pod space was probably as confining. The magnificent six were no more ... separated, or lost forever.

Three warm stalks suddenly plucked the third pea from the receptacle and placed it in a small pod-like container, along with a handful of other peas. From their vantage point, they could clearly see a large blue pod in the distance. The strange pod had a top to it, below which a fluffy white substance billowed. It reminded the third pea of the objects that sometimes passed the expanse of blue, which he'd spied through his pod. This substance didn't look nearly as harmless and the third pea felt pangs of impending danger. Why had they been selected, segregated and cast to one side?

The alien with the stalks picked up the large container and its inmates. Another identical alien lifted the lid from the pod that contained the fluffy substance. The third pea could feel a surge of heat emanating from the bubbling pod. The air was thick with jumbled, confused and frightened thoughts, as the doomed peas were poured into the pod and the top slammed shut. The thoughts gradually faded away, leaving an eerie silence in its wake. The surviving peas knew that their friends were no more and that their final moments must have been truly horrifying. They couldn't imagine a fate worse than that which they had just witnessed.

Mere moments passed before the remaining peas would know what was in store for them. Cradled in a set of five closely knit stalks, the peas were carried to a place where the surface was dirty and of a similar colour to Geoff's flesh, when last the third pea had seen it.

The surviving peas were laid on the dirt. An alien used a single stalk to bore a hole deep into the surface of the dirt. The peas waited as this process was repeated over and over, until there were the same number of holes as there were peas. Three rows and eight holes to a row. Is there no mercy, thought the third pea, as their destiny became fearfully apparent to them all.

One by one, a pea was selected and deposited into the newly prepared ground. As each was dropped, so it was covered; buried alive by an alien being, in an alien world.

The last pea to be buried was the third pea and, as the dirt was filled in from above, thoughts of better times eased the pain. "I spy with my little eye something beginning with..."

THREE BAR

The room is stale with cigarette smoke. A small steel table and three sturdy pine chairs are all that prevents it from being an empty room. A light bulb hangs naked from the ceiling, illuminating the solitary occupant of one chair, casting harsh shadows of table and chair. There is no window, but the steel door has a small external sliding viewing panel, offering an outsider's glimpse of the scene within. Bagged brick walls coated with dirty white, blistered paint feed little damp mounds of flaky grey matter onto the bare concrete floor.

A trail of tiny red ants enter and exit minute cracks between wall, floor and paint deposits. Small volcanic mounds of orange sand erupt along a fault-line crack in the floor, as larger black ants go about their business uninterrupted.

The man in the chair sits motionless and hunched, his grey stubbled cheeks resting between his leathery palms. His elbows ache under the weight they carry and his head throbs with the weight of the problem he faces – a problem that is not of his own doing and a problem for which there is no apparent answer.

How many times over the past three weeks has he thought about that day? If only he could turn back the clock to the day before. If only he could stop thinking about turning back the clock, which, although gave him temporary relief, invariably brought him crashing back to reality with the force of a sledgehammer blow to the stomach.

Gordon Stevens "had it good", as he was constantly reminded by one of his regular four-ball friends at Atlantic Beach Golf Club. Senior partner with Stevens, Bauer, Lukehurst & Associates, he was one of the top attorneys in Cape Town and had recently bought a second home up the coast on the golf estate he'd been a member of for the last ten years. It was a snip at "three bar", and a little insider knowledge of a deceased estate the firm had been handling had made the transaction even more satisfying. Gordon loved a bargain and the golf estate home at the club was exactly that. He also loved talking about wealth … his wealth, and referring to everything in "bar" really gave him a buzz. That convertible he'd recently bought his wife had set him back "over a bar", information that he volunteered quite readily when friends had visited their Constantia home recently.

The steel door of the room in which Gordon had been placed squeaks and then rings out as a bolt is wiggled and then suddenly withdrawn. Keys are sorted on the other side and inserted into the lock. A man with the keys reshuffles the pack, mutters some incomprehensible words and the door is successfully unlocked at his second attempt. Gordon raises his head and drops his arms to the side of the chair. His silver hair is greasy and swept back and high on his head from constant nervous finger combing. Bloodshot eyes disguise the blue that once had golf club wives and office secretaries chattering in the ladies'.

The man with the keys was a familiar sight to the captive. Uniformed and stereotypical of the Latino policeman, he wore his horseshoe moustache with pride and, had he smiled, the world would see his gold-capped front tooth – a sure sign that he also "had it good". Dark glasses completed the look and his holstered gun was more visible than necessary, fastened high on his waist, just in case anyone needed reminding. He stood at the doorway, allowing two plain-clothed men to enter, before stepping inside and closing the door behind him. Had there been another chair, he'd not have taken it. His place was to stand sentry and guard the unlocked door. He sucked a tooth … one or two down from the gold one, part of which was now visible through his thick black moustache and chapped bottom lip.

The two men each took a chair. One man spun his around one-eighty and sat "cop-style" with arms folded on top of the chair back, while the other took a more conventional, but nevertheless well-rehearsed position, slightly behind and just to one side, as a second line of defence. They, too, were playing their role. Casually dressed in grey trousers, black shoes and white shirts with sleeves rolled up high to the bicep, the main man has yellow sweat stains to the armpits and one frayed collar with a slightly protruding plastic collar stiffener. Both men were unshaven and both had self-rolled cigarettes hanging loosely from thin narrow lips.

Olive loved her new home on the estate at Atlantic Beach. Although not in her name, it was the perfect place from which she could pop into town to shop at the Waterfront or lunch with her friends in Long Street. At twenty-seven, she was doing all right – a small monthly allowance to supplement her part-time modelling assignments was handy, but she felt Gordon could dig a little deeper if she was to be truly contented. To appease her, Gordon had promised to put the house in her name "a little down the line".

"Not too far down the line," she'd prompted. Not bad for the girl who dropped out of school early, got caught up in drugs and shoplifting and for a while looked to be heading for some serious jail time. Luckily for her, her grandmother's savings and a sympathetic senior partner at SBL & Associates had saved her neck. The hourly rate he paid her for filing was ridiculously low, but he did like to do his bit for the community, which is how he related the story at Atlantic Beach.

She'd been indebted to her shining knight, Mr Stevens … very indebted indeed. After the trial was over they'd met in his office for what Gordon had termed a "debriefing". A few days later over lunch, Mr Stevens became Gordon. Lunches became dinners and dinners became beds ... Gordon became Gordy and Mrs Stevens remained oblivious. The beds were randomly chosen and rarely the same. Four-star hotels and guesthouses were booked to coincide with briefings in Johannesburg, Durban and other "up-country" destinations.

Gordon's golfing friends were aware of Olive. How could they not be? Gordon hadn't exactly been discreet about her. She was always at prize-giving and now that meant Wednesday afternoons in addition to the regular Saturday afternoon competitions. Gordon would drive up on Friday evening after the traffic had eased a little, and then drive back on Sunday.

Elizabeth Stevens loathed golf, the windy Atlantic coast and, more recently, she'd begun to loathe her husband, who spent an ever-increasing amount of time with his golfing buddies. At weekends and now mid-week, she was left her alone in their rambling Constantia manor house. At fifty, the torment of being childless was a distant, but still painful memory that burned her inner core. Close friends' children were now having their own children and the wounds deep within Elizabeth were reopened once more with every tale of refurbished cots, embroidered Christmas stockings and paddling-pool photos.

Big boys' weekend away trips to international rugby matches could only be topped by golfing tours to faraway destinations. Clive had proposed it, Martin seconded it and Gordon had volunteered his secretary's services to organise it. Before long, they had the required eight names inked in for their ten-day golfing tour of Argentina, which was Clive's country of choice and, after all, he'd suggested the tour. And if they could all agree on the dates, they could combine their golf with a Springboks vs Pumas rugby match.

The line of questioning had been the same for the last three weeks. Different people asking, but always the same questions. Some could hardly speak English, but were well practised, while others embellished the questions with little irrelevant asides, asking if Gordon wanted a cigarette or water. The former wasn't wanted and the later was denied.

"Who gave you the consignment?"

"Where were you taking it and who was to receive it?"

"How many times have you done this in other countries?"

"If you didn't pack your own bag, then why did you say that you had?"

"Who gave you the consignment?"

"Where were you taking it and who was to receive it?

Over and over … the same questions. Sometimes the frequency would change … rapid fire, hot, stale, smoker's breath, spitting out the words an inch from Gordon's face, or right into his ear. Sometimes there would be a minute, maybe two between questions; seconds between words, soft … loud … but always the same questions.

The tour had not even got underway. It was cut short at the Ministro Pistarini international airport customs department in Buenos Aires. After some interrogation, the remaining seven golfers had been put on the first available plane back to South Africa, without the option of continuing with their vacation – not that they would have wanted to had they been given the choice. The newspapers had hold of the story and the whole saga was a bloody mess. Between four to sixteen years, that's what was reported and that's what the embassy representative had told him.

"Probably eight to ten for 350g" is what his appointed lawyer had told him, depending on how he pleaded. Yes, everyone is innocent … everyone.

Gordon had sent for his own representative, but he was still waiting – Myles Truscott, top dog.

After two, or maybe five hours, Gordon was led back to his cell. Similarly decorated to the interview room, his cell was much smaller, but at least had a tiny high-level opening that provided some miserly ventilation to the room which, much to Gordon's surprise and relief, he shared with no one. A concrete bench acted as seat and bed. Gordon gazed up at the window opening and counted the heavy vertical metal bars that prevented escape through a gap no bigger than his briefcase.

"One, two, three," he whispered quietly to himself. It was a three-bar cell, a thousand miles from Atlantic Beach with a window the size of a barmaid's tray.

A month or two earlier, Elizabeth Stevens had been posting Facebook photos, updating this and down loading that, when a temporary power outage had her marching to the bedroom, to see if her husband had left his laptop at home, as was sometimes the case. He hadn't, which infuriated her even more. However, he had forgotten to take his briefcase to work. He never forgot his briefcase and would surely be phoning her to bring it through, or sending some spotty office minion through to collect it. Although she'd had the opportunity to go through his private case before, she'd never had the inclination or desire to do so ... until that day. She didn't know what compelled her, but with a dexterity derived from her teenage record-browsing years, Elizabeth Stevens picked her way through dossiers, affidavits, title deeds and ... title deeds? What was Gordon doing concerning himself with title deeds? That was article clerk's work, spotty office minion stuff. She sifted through the Atlantic paper trail piece by piece, document upon document, probably destined for the office, but carelessly temporarily filed in a briefcase.

Atlantic Beach Estate ... three million two hundred and twenty thousand rand. Transferred from a Mr James to a Miss Olive June

Parsons aged twenty-bloody-seven - but paid for, by all accounts by her fifty-five-year-old son-of-a-bitch husband.

Elizabeth resisted the temptation to throw anything anywhere, shout expletives at the gods, or confront her husband by phone or in person, should he arrive to collect his work. Ten minutes later and a spotty minion duly arrived to be his master's voice and collect his master's briefcase. That Wednesday afternoon, as Gordon tee-ed it up on the first, Elizabeth had finished her second bottle of her favourite Moreson "Miss Molly" Cabernet Sauvignon Merlot blend.

"Good golly," she slurred ... then giggled.

"Good golly Miss Molly, Good golly Miss ... Parsons," she sobbed.

By the time Elizabeth had spilled the entire third bottle of red on her carpet and emptied half a bottle of Southern Comfort down her throat, she was far from comforted. The temptation was irresistible and the remaining half bottle slammed into the chest of drawers and accompanying wedding photos.

Gordon had shot a seventy-eight, collected a meat hamper and a bottle of plonk for best net score of the day and he was about to tee up Olive on the king-size duvet overlooking their Table Mountain backdrop. The southeaster was pumping, sending misty clouds of mystery cascading down towards Table Bay. Gordon, Olive and their mountain were as one – rolling, tumbling and swirling from heady heights to sublime submission and fulfilled tranquillity.

Gordon had bought the Atlantic Beach house for Olive and although the title deeds were in her name, he'd withheld all of the details, preferring to offer her little titbits now and then. It gave him a "three bar" buzz to tell her at first that she could visit the house. But as her appetite grew, so he was required to throw out a few more morsels upon which she could feed. Sure, she could live there. She could live there and maybe, just maybe he would give it to her one day. Okay, he would give it to her soon. Next, he was busy with the paperwork.

As the sun set over the Atlantic that Wednesday evening, Olive lay spoon to spoon with Gordon, his head propped up on two pillows, so both could see the boiling red globe of gasses turn orange, elongate, submit and quietly slip into the sea.

Gordon was a spent force with no more to give … nothing but the last piece in a complex puzzle. To his surprise, Olive's reaction was unexpected. She was neither excited, nor ungrateful. She seemed contented, perhaps a hint of relief.

But Olive was more than relieved. She had a house on the estate that cost "just over three bar", but was by all accounts (if bar talk could be trusted) worth about eight. She didn't trust bar talk, but a local estate agent had given her a conservative six and a half.

She turned to Gordon and slid her leg up and over his thigh. Her leg nestled firmly above his hip and she pulled his body closer with her heel to the small of his back, whilst pushing his upper body from hers. She tugged his hair with clenched fists and pulled his head firmly into her breasts.

"I don't know how I can ever thank you enough, Gordy ... but I'll try – as best I can."

Even with the best lawyer in town, Gordon knew that his fate was inevitable; it was just a question of time. A question of time, he thought to himself. Five, ten, fifteen? Even as an unwitting "mule", the penalties were stiff. He'd been advised to concoct a plausible story whereby he could plead guilty in the hope of a more lenient sentence, as the courts came down heavy on those who persisted with their turn of events, which invariably involved a trip to the toilet and unattended luggage, or that friendly stranger who offered to watch the bag in exchange for transporting a parcel through customs ... he would do it himself, but it contains perfume for his sister and he's already over his allowance with the Chanel No. 5 his wife wanted.

Three hundred grams in his briefcase! Gordon put his head in his hands, as he'd done so often for the past twenty-odd days. A tear rolled swiftly down his hand and fell from his wrist onto the warm concrete floor, where it winced and recoiled against the dusty, sandy veneer that was Gordon's carpet.

Why the hell had he taken his brief case on a golf trip, anyway? He thought it would impress the rest of the party to be on holiday, yet so in demand, that work was always just a click away, a necessity … just one step away from his office, which could barely survive without him. His laptop would have done that … so why on earth take the briefcase? But he always took his briefcase, everywhere – he knew that. Only he and Elizabeth knew that!

Myles Truscott arrived the next morning. He met with Gordon in the same interview room, guarded by the same gold-toothed warder, who sucked the same tooth with same annoying regularity. Myles had been digging and had assigned his own senior minions to dig on his and Gordon's behalf. Elizabeth had known about Olive for some time, in fact some considerable time.

Myles left Gordon with little hope of a successful outcome to the impending trial. It would be swift, it would be chaotic and it would be anything but sweet … unlike his wife's revenge. She'd had little to say to Myles that afternoon and certainly nothing that Gordon would wish to hear. Through her drunken tirade he'd picked up enough to know that she'd gone through his files, followed up on a few very traceable leads and unravelled the truth about Olive, and several other infidelities along the way.

Gordon got off relatively lightly. His divorce went through during his second year of an eight-year prison term, which he'd been told would probably mean only five at most, though gone was his single-occupancy cell, embassy staff   visits and three-bar window. The dim light was artificial and ventilation nonexistent. The noise and stench were unbearable.

Olive put her house on the market with the same local estate agent, received her asking price of seven bar and moved into a three-bar flat in Cape Town, where she reunited with old friends, reignited embers with old flames and bought fifty grams of shit from the same supplier of the three hundred gram consignment that had delivered her from the clutches of "that revolting old man up the coast".

She had it good.

WALTER

Lifting his bum just an inch or two off his modified baby seat enabled Walter to survey the scene outside. The action was not without its consequences. The safety belt cut into the thin flesh on his shoulder and a spasm shot through his back, as if poked in the kidneys by a fully charged cattle prod. The last thing he needed at five in the morning was another reminder of the congenital spine disorder that plagued the most mundane of daily routines. Sock-less feet and Velcro-fastened shoes had enabled him to dress in the morning for the past few years. Toenails were cut in a steamy hot bath tub, when sinews and vertebrae were loose and off guard.

He arched his back and gave up on the sightseeing; not that there was much to see in the Western Cape at that time of the morning and at that time of the year. July school holidays had come upon them again and with that came a timely reminder of the perils of urban driving in the early hours of a Saturday morning, as a Golf GTi took them on the inside lane … no lights, bass beat pumping and doing about one-sixty. He cast a glance at the driver beside him. Eric always took the middle lane given a choice of three, even on a road devoid of any traffic. Walter had once suggested he move over and he did, into the right-hand lane.

"Night clubs are spilling out then, Eric," Walter said, easing the tedium of an eight-hour journey with a little light conversation.

"Arseholes!" replied Eric and that was that for the time being.

Eric was the straight guy in their circus routine. His performance was like his driving – middle of the road, nothing too edgy. His wife of thirty years, Flo, was in the following convoy, probably third out of the seven pantechnicons and assorted towed caravans that were the Bingham Brothers' Circus entourage. They never travelled together, Eric preferring the company of his comedy act partner and Flo preferring the company of anyone but Eric.

"You're just like an ugly Clark Gable, but not quite," Flo had once said of him long ago, when they were on speaking terms.

"Not quite what?" Eric had asked "Not quite like that at all, or not quite as ugly as an ugly Clark Gable?" He never got an answer, but that didn't worry him, as he wasn't too sure who Clark Gable was anyway. He was as tall as Walter was short and the parting in his greased-down, jet-black hair was like his driving and his acting: middle of the road. Walter glanced up at his truck-driver friend. Jet-black hair didn't look good on a sixty-year-old. Nor did his John Lennon glasses and grey moustache, but who was he to judge another by his looks, even if he did look older than he should. The five years between them looked more like fifteen, but people often had trouble with Walter's age. Even strangers would have no compunction in announcing "You dwarfs all look the same to me." Walter had given up telling them that he wasn't a dwarf and would invariably prefer to just waddle off whistling hi-ho, hi-ho.

Sun Valley was their traditional July stopover and had been for as long as anyone could remember. The small shopping centre had a vacant spot between it and the main road, just big enough for a "Big Top" tent, or in the case of Bingham Brothers, more of a "Medium Top" awning supported by an array of gum poles, rectangular steel sections and scaffolding.

By six o'clock they had pulled into their site, sunrise still a coffee cup or two away. Walter clambered down the outside of the truck as he'd become accustomed, jumping the last foot or two into the darkness and landing in a shallow muddy puddle.

Generators fired up enough light for animals to be unloaded for a stretch and munch on the grass. Livestock comprised a juvenile elephant, which could stand on hind legs, three Shetland ponies that ran around the straw bales demarcating the ring. First they ran this way and then they ran that - they did little else but that run around and look cute to every six-year-old girl whose parents paid the price of a ticket. A handful of poodles completed the animal acts, leaping through hoops and into the open arms of their trainer Flo, who imparted all her love and cuddles on her "little babies". That was when she wasn't imparting all her love and cuddles on the only surviving Bingham brother. Jean and Peter had left older brother Bill Bingham to it ten years earlier, telling him that they'd take a fraction of their share because the show wouldn't last another season.

"Why do we always arrive in the dark, offload in the dark, erect in the dark and then sit down and wait all day for the afternoon performance?" asked Walter, as he and Eric sat on beer crates dunking rusks into their tin mugs of sickly sweet coffee.

"Because Bingham's an arsehole," said Eric, dropping half a soggy rusk into his mug and splashing his shirt. At four foot six Walter's shoes didn't even touch the ground, but at least his shirt was dry and clean. Walter dug around in his trouser pocket and popped a couple of painkillers into his coffee.

"Got any new ideas for the show, Eric?" asked the little guy with the bald head and shaven eyebrows. There were a few strands of hair on top that required the occasional razor cut. His hair was grey but grown a foot and a half down his back. He hadn't needed a clown hairpiece since his early thirties. God, it had been Walter & Eric for over thirty years.

"Thirty fucking years, Eric. Thirty fucking years," he said, "and we haven't changed the routine a bit in all that time. What does that tell you, Eric? What does that say to you?"

"We're arseholes?"

"Sad arseholes, Eric. We're a couple of sad mothers," Walter said, as he swung off the crate and headed towards his caravan, calling after his friend over his shoulder. "Fancy a dop? It is after midday somewhere in the world, after all."

The two men sat on Walter's bunk bed and cracked open a bottle of Klipdrift brandy, which was poured generously into their unwashed tin mugs. It was eight o'clock.

"Cheers, old boy," said the midget.

"Your very good health, sir," replied Eric in what he thought was a pucker British upper-crust accent, before clinking mugs and downing his drink in three gulps. "Don't mind if I do," he said, filling his mug once more.

Walter's aged black cat purred at his feet, unable to make the leap to his bed. Walter sympathised with his pet's physical inability to do what his mind wanted. He heaved a little grunt as he got off the bed and back again, holding Sputnik in his arms and muttering his name into the little white patch under the cat's chin.

"Why'd you call him Sputnik, Walter?"

"Sputnik was the name of the early Russian space ships, Eric," he replied. "You know," sending out a little lure to his friend, who he sensed was slowly mulling over the answer in his mind. Walter could see the cogs turning and enjoyed the moment. It wasn't the answer that could warrant his usual a-hole response, so none was forthcoming.

Walter's drinking and pill popping accounted for most of his income. Food was secondary and usually appeared from someone at some time during the day. He didn't really need food and a hot dog or burger a day usually did the trick. If he didn't get food, there was always a bottle of 'Klippies' to serve up for dinner. The down side was not only his health, but also his pocket. His meagre earnings from the circus barely covered his painkillers, downers, uppers, sleepers and booze. He'd just have to do what he always did at Sun Valley Mall and others like it all over the country.

"Can I speak to Mike, please" he politely asked the frumpy peroxide blonde who answered the door to the Centre Manager's office. Walter took a long red balloon from behind his back, which he'd blown up and tied before knocking at the door. Mike, the Centre Manager, usually gave him a hundred rand a morning to entertain the local kids in the Mall and he got to keep the five rand he charged for turning a couple of pieces of floppy rubber into a giraffe or horse.

"Mike who?" asked the woman, looking down her nose at the midget before her, squeaking his nasty balloons in his dirty little mits … and that hair!

"Mike, the manager," said Walter mid dog. He stopped his twisting and tweaking.

"That's not going to happen," she snapped. "He left six months ago and I'm the Centre Manager … ess," she added, with a hiss to round off her dismissal.

"But, I mean, can I … "

"We don't need your type here," she said coldly. Walter's expression begged the question and she offered the answer. "Gypsies!" she said, slamming the door firmly in his face.

Walter made his way back to his caravan site, where work was going on full steam for the matinee show, due to commence at two that afternoon. His three hours of balloon work were history, so he continued with the book he'd started the previous week – The Glass Bead Game by Hermann Hesse. Money was going to be a major problem now. Maybe they would put bums on seats, with capacity audiences of three hundred – every day for three weeks and twice on weekends. Then Mr Bingham would give them all a bonus. Bloody woman, he thought. Arsehole.

Walter sat at his seat, in front of the mirror he'd been staring into for the last thirty-odd years.

"Mirror, mirror on the wall, who's the funniest of them all?" he said out loud.

"You are, Mitzi. You are the funniest of them all," he replied in falsetto voice, a little pre make-up ritual he'd enacted for … for … thirty fucking years.

First the foundation, from bald spot to Adam's apple and everything in between. Big dark rings around his bloodshot eyes and a bright wide-lipped smiley mouth, in contrast to the two teardrops falling from one eye. His eye brows were applied with eye-liner … one pointing skyward, the other dipping low and a large bright tomato nose to round it all off. He'd studied the classic clown masks from the early days of Fratellini, Grimaldi and others. He'd copied Coco for a while before settling on his own mask. It was Mitzi's face and Mitzi's persona. A costume of silky chequer patterns and yellow polka dots, size-eighteen lightweight red shoes fastened with Velcro and a pink bowler hat with an arrow through the head were all his trademarks and the children loved him. It was time to sneak a peek and check out the ticket sales. Half an hour to go, so there should be a steady stream by now.

Walter walked in full costume from his caravan to the rear of the tent, avoiding a large pile of elephant dung and the same puddle from his early-morning dip. He pressed his nose to a gap in the canvas and counted. Eight, nine … nine … nine. That was it. Ten, eleven, twelve, as a mother and twins entered on the far side.

It was half past two and ringmaster Bingham was playing brinkmanship to its finest. How long could he delay the start for late arrivals, before the early birds wanted their money back and started to leave?

"Ladies, gentleman, boy and girls, welcome to Bingham Brothers' greatest show on earth." Half of the thirty-strong audience offered muted applause to a backdrop of a crying toddler in the front row, his mother doing her best to placate him.

"Arsehole," said Eric, peering through the same gap, but three feet higher than Walter, who was watching the spectacle below him. They were waiting their cue. After the horses and before the jugglers, then after the dogs and once more for the finalé. They marked time with a bottle of Government House port, which was finished just in time for them to pick up a few props and wait for the departure of the Shetlands. Being the surprise act, they got no ringmaster's introduction.

"One, two, three," said Walter and in they went. The bucket of pretend water, which actually held confetti, the slap on the head with a plastic cod and the inevitable kick in the pants for the straight guy were all going well, until Walter tripped and landed on the bucket. It wasn't part of their routine, but nobody noticed and it got a few laughs. Even Eric thought his pal had varied the act for the better. Only Walter's bleeding shin bone and grimace would have given it away, but each was concealed under blood-red baggies and thick mascara.

The act went off as it had always done, but each season drew fewer laughs, as the delights of video games and a severe shortage of parental spare change sucked the life out of Bingham Brothers greatest show on earth. Twenty-two people had paid and there may just be enough in the till the next morning for animal fodder, fuel and not much else.

Mr Bingham called everyone together at five o'clock that afternoon for a meeting under the big top. What he told them was not the usual Bingham rally cry of "times are tough and we need to work on our acts to get the crowds flooding back". This was a very subdued Bingham before them. He looked a beaten man, the weight of time and responsibility heavy on his shoulders. There had been a Bingham Brothers' Circus for nearly ninety years. But that was all to end. There would be no more shows after this short season. In three weeks' time, the elephant would go to a nearby private game park. They'd had offers for the ponies and Flo would keep "her babies". He had a plan for everyone and everything. He would cut his losses and live in retirement on the funds he had squirrelled away all these years. There were no lines to read between, as the path was laid out in front of them. Solholi pivate game park, just a few kilometres away on the road to Ocean View, would take the elephants. That's why they were finishing up here … a convenient drop-off point.

Walter and Eric said nothing on leaving the tent. Nobody said a word. In three weeks' time they would all go their separate ways … jobless and hopeless.

"Who wants a fifty-five-year old midget clown in this day and age," Walter said to his mirror, before making up for the evening show.

Forty-one people attended in the evening. Less than expected and not enough to force a change of the owner's heart. The finalé came and went, as did Walter and Eric, back to the caravan. They passed Bingham on the way.

"Arsehole," said Eric.

"Arsehole," echoed Walter.

The two clowns sat on Walter's bunk, as they had done so many times before. They drank a bottle of Klippies and had a stupid row about something innocuous to do with Sputnik. Eric left in a drunken stupor.

Walter sat at his mirror, cotton wool and cream in hand. He wiped a streaky diagonal smudge across his face, mingling red lips, white cheeks and black eyes. One tear remained on the other cheek, before being scythed in two by real salty tears streaming down his face. Sputnik looked up at his master, as he placed a bottle of Old Brown Sherry on the small shelf under the mirror.

"Mirror, mirror on the wall. Who the fuck are you?"

Walter counted out the little red and green pills in the child-proof bottle, then the white tablets he kept in shoe box of photos next to his bed. Some sleepers. No, all of the sleepers. He sat on his chair and mixed them all up and then put them in batches of six before him. Fourteen batches of six … fourteen handfuls of Smarties, all washed down with Old Brown Sherry. Walter gazed at the mirror in front of him once more.

"Mirror, mirror," he said. "Mirror, mirror, mirror … arsehole mirror." He staggered to his feet and lay on his bunk bed, muttering to himself as he fell into a deep, deep sleep. " Mirr…or, mirror."

ABOUT THE AUTHOR

Simon Humphreys was born and educated in the UK, but now lives in Noordhoek, Cape Town, where he has his own Quantity Surveying company.

He enjoys playing veterans hockey and sailing his 1938 boat "Quest" in the waters of False Bay.

His Cup of Tea won first place in the Global Short Stories competition in 2012. Askance Publishing have included Sandman and Service Delivery in their short story anthologies. Trenches appears in Twisted Tales 2014.

His vegetable garden inspired his story The Third Pea.

RAGING AARDVARK PUBLICATIONS

Raging Aardvark Publications is an Australian indie publisher which promotes creative artists of edgy, off-kilter work in anthologies of short stories, flash fiction and poetry, as well as delving into non-fiction.

They are committed to sourcing a wide range of cross-genre fiction which not only pushes the boundaries, but stirs the emotions of their readers.

Non-fiction themes explore living an authentic life, balancing the challenges of the 21st Century and exploring the vast range of experiences within relationships.

Raging Aardvark supports International Flash Fiction Day through an extensive competition culminating in the anthology "Twisted Tales".

As their literary imprint, Cats With Thumbs, they produce a blogzine biannually. The annual anthology of favourite poetry, short stories, artwork and photography is published in July.

Titles available from Amazon include:

Choose your Adventures – written by a number of authors

History's Keeper

Dust and Death

Zombie Now

Anthologies involving a number of authors

New Sun Rising – Stories for Japan

Twisted Tales 2012 – Flash Fiction with a Twist

Twisted Tales 2013 – Flash Fiction with a Twist

Twisted Tales 2014 – Flash Fiction with a Twist

Twisted Tales 2015 – Flash Fiction with a Twist

Cats With Thumbs, 2015

Single author anthologies

Consuming the Muse – erotic tales – AstridL

Mercury Blobs – Sylvia Petter

Love just is – Kate Murray

Shadows Close – Kate Murray

Sandman - Simon Humphreys

Non Fiction

Reclaim – Sex after Birth – Annie Evett

It's up to Me – Warren Hooke

Upcoming Titles

Raunchy Recipes – Erotic tales blended with a recipe – Anthology

Anthology – Sartres' Lonely Toybox – Annie Evett

Brother Dragon and Racoon walk the Camino – Annie Evett

Letters to Saffy – Kiki Jarrott

For more information, check our website.

http://ragingaardvark.com

www.ingramcontent.com/pod-product-compliance
Lightning Source LLC
Chambersburg PA
CBHW031309120626
46554CB00001BA/348